"Why is it I can remember an old movie, but I can't remember my own name?"

Mac asked. "And why did the doctor call me Mr. Charles?"

"Because that's what I told him," Melanie stated, as calmly as she could.

"I don't understand."

She sighed. "I hope you won't be angry, but I, uh, let you believe certain things last night that weren't exactly true."

His dark eyes narrowed slightly. "About what?"

"About us."

"Us?"

"Actually, Mac, I know that I let you believe we were sort of . . . well, together . . . but the truth is that we just met."

An expression very close to shock crossed his handsome face. "I don't believe it."

Dear Reader,

Welcome to Silhouette—experience the magic of the wonderful world where two people fall in love. Meet heroines who will make you cheer for their happiness, and heroes (be they the boy next door or a handsome, mysterious stranger) who will win your heart. Silhouette Romance reflects the magic of love—sweeping you away with books that will make you laugh and cry, heartwarming, poignant stories that will move you time and time again.

In the coming months we're publishing romances by many of your all-time favorites, such as Diana Palmer, Brittany Young, Sondra Stanford and Annette Broadrick. Your response to these authors and our other Silhouette Romance authors has served as a touchstone for us, and we're pleased to bring you more books with Silhouette's distinctive medley of charm, wit and—above all—*romance*.

I hope you enjoy this book and the many stories to come. Experience the magic!

Sincerely,

Tara Hughes
Senior Editor
Silhouette Books

PATRICIA ELLIS

Sweet Protector

Silhouette Romance

Published by Silhouette Books New York

America's Publisher of Contemporary Romance

To Mom, for always saying,
"I don't know why you don't write,
you've always been good at that."

SILHOUETTE BOOKS
300 E. 42nd St., New York, N.Y. 10017

ISBN: 0-373-08684-9

First Silhouette Books printing November 1989

Printed in the U.S.A.

PATRICIA ELLIS

was born in Detroit to parents from central Mississippi. Being bicultural probably contributed to her wanderlust and her love of travel, along with an incurable sense of curiosity. An actress at heart, she studied theater and acting at college but found that writing came just as naturally. Currently she is dividing her time between reading and writing romantic novels and working toward her Ph.D. in theater history.

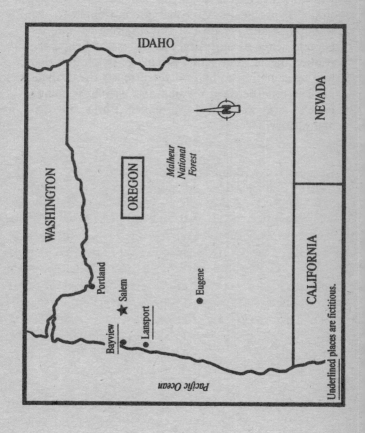

Chapter One

There he was. He was tall, about six-one or two, she decided. Dark brown hair that looked thick enough to walk through. Melanie sighed. Who was he? She may not have known all of the people in town, but she recognized most of them, and he certainly was not a local. Not that he wasn't familiar. This was the third time she had seen him. The first time had been when he had whizzed past her on the highway in a black sports car and had waved at her. Which had caused her to swerve and just miss running off the road. The second time was in a local department store. She had been on the up escalator, and he had been on the down. He had winked at her, and after they had passed each other, she had not been able to resist turning and sneaking a peek. He had turned around and had been staring at her. She had tripped when the escalator reached the top. He had laughed at her. Now Melanie laughed at herself and adjusted the telephoto lens on her camera.

He was certainly the best-looking man she had ever seen. He seemed very self-confident, and she wondered if he knew how sexy he was. Probably. And that would spoil the effect, rendering him less sexy in her eyes. However, since she was still gazing at him from afar—or at least from across the street—she could maintain her illusions about his personality. She wasn't sure why she was so preoccupied with him. Normally, Melanie Rogers was not a man chaser. As she readjusted the lens, she reminded herself that she was not chasing, but merely watching. An acceptable spectator sport for anyone.

"Hi."

Melanie jumped and dropped the camera, which was secured around her neck by a wide Indian-design strap. She turned to stare down at a six-year-old face with several dirt streaks on it. The park was flooded with children who had been released from school for the summer, and Melanie knew most of them. She smiled at the child with the bright red hair and a face full of freckles.

"Hi, Beth. Are you glad school is out?"

The child continued to look across the street at where Melanie had been focusing her camera and nodded. The man was standing outside the telegraph office at a newsstand, buying a Portland newspaper.

"What're you doing, Mel'nie?"

As she smiled at the version of her name, Melanie pointed at the old movie theater across from them, several storefronts down from the telegraph office. "I'm taking pictures of the Strand because I'm writing a story about it for the paper."

The little girl looked at the theater and then looked at the man at the newsstand, who was now getting into a sleek black Jaguar. "If you were taking pictures of the theater, why were you pointing your camera over there?" A small grubby finger pointed at the newsstand. Melanie sighed.

"I was just taking pictures of the whole block, Beth."

"Uh-huh."

So the kid didn't believe her. What should she have said? *I was checking out that fantastic-looking man and wondering who he is and if I will ever get a chance to meet him and find out if his personality matches his looks?* Her horoscope had told her she would be meeting the man of her dreams this week. Of course, it had been telling her that, off and on, for the past four years.

Melanie knew all the available men in the small town of Bayview. Her sister and brother-in-law had blatantly run every single man within a fifty-mile radius by her and refused to give up when she had politely rejected them all. Melanie didn't know who she was waiting for, but she knew that none of them had been the one for her. The people in town seemed to have accepted the fact that Melanie was a career woman, and probably, she thought, some believed that if she ever found a man she wouldn't know what to do with him.

Melanie knew what she would do with him. She read *Cosmo*. She also knew that the majority of the population of Bayview—some 15,300 souls—thought she was going to end up an embittered old maid. Not that it bothered her. What people thought about her had never particularly mattered to Melanie.

She realized that she was having a staredown with a six-year-old. Fortunately, Beth's mother called her, and the child departed. Melanie glanced at her watch and repacked her camera. She would have to take the rest of the pictures later; she was late. Melanie ran over to her small red Escort and jumped in, placing the camera bag next to her. She sped down the street of the square and then turned off onto the road that led to the new development that had been built just outside the downtown area.

Fifteen years earlier the city of Bayview had been deteriorating from the inside out, with the young people leaving
to seek well-paying jobs in larger cities like Portland and
Salem. The town's population had been dwindling, and the
lack of taxpayers had shown on the shabby storefronts on
the square.

Then Frank Wilson had moved WilCom to Bayview. The
computer industry was booming, and WilCom had brought
that boom to Bayview, pumping money and hope into the
town and its people. Suddenly, people didn't have to leave
to get good jobs, and other businesses started settling there
as well. Now Bayview had a shopping mall, two drive-in
theaters and several good restaurants. The downtown area
was getting a face-lift from shopkeepers, who finally had
enough money to maintain the century old buildings.

Melanie had pulled into the WilCom parking lot and was
striding toward the building when she saw the Jaguar parked
in the next row. Her stomach tightened in anticipation. He
was here. Maybe now she would find out who he was.

Melanie walked over and stood behind the expensive automobile. Oregon license plates. So, he was at least from the
same state. If he was conducting business with WilCom,
Liane would know about it, and Melanie planned to pump
her about him over lunch. Her sister wouldn't like it, but
only because she hadn't seen him first. Poor Liane really
had a matchmaking complex. Melanie smiled to herself.
This time, she wouldn't mind.

The summer sun glinted off the windows of the WilCom
Building, and as she opened the door and felt the welcom-
ing coolness of the air-conditioning, Melanie glanced at the
sporty watch on her wrist and punched the elevator button.
She was only a few minutes late. Maybe Liane wouldn't notice. The doors of the elevator slid open on the top floor,
and Melanie stepped off onto the thick carpeting and walked

the few feet to where her sister sat behind the receptionist's desk. Liane looked up and smiled.

"Well, only four minutes late. What is this, a new leaf?"

Melanie laughed at the joke about her perpetual tardiness and decided not to use any of her perfectly valid excuses since Liane had already heard them all.

"Yes, well, just be thankful you have me. Are you ready?"

Liane grinned and glanced over at a closed conference room door. She then pulled her purse out of a desk drawer.

"Actually, I'm not. I have to go to the ladies' room. You can watch the phones until Jackie gets here. Hey, that's a sharp outfit. Where did you get that hat?"

Melanie glanced down at the lightweight white jumpsuit with the red piping and then looked up at the brim of the matching red-and-white straw hat and laughed.

"I just decided to buy myself a present. Like it?"

Liane nodded and strode down the hall, saying she would be back in a minute.

Melanie leaned against the front of the desk and crossed her ankles. Her white high-heeled sandals were from last year, but they looked like they had been bought to go with the outfit. Her red purse with its long, thin strap made her feel as if she had been "put together" at a department store. Her flare for fashion had always confused Liane. One day Melanie would be wearing old jeans, a ragged sweatshirt and leather boots, and the next day a silk dress with coordinated accessories. Melanie had discovered that there was no one style that was "her," so she dressed according to how she felt each day.

Even though Liane was nine years older than Melanie, the sisters were close, as they were to their two brothers. Clay and Jeremy were living in Portland now, but they kept in touch. Since the death of their parents in an automobile accident three years earlier, Liane had become the unofficial head of the family. It was only in recent months that she had also become a mother hen to her siblings.

Melanie heard the door to the conference room to her right open, and as people began filing out into the hall, the phone beeped. Executive phones never rang—they beeped. Melanie twisted her torso and picked up the phone.

"Good afternoon, Mr. Wilson's office. May I help you?"

As she listened to the man on the telephone, she saw Frank Wilson, president of WilCom, three of his executives and *the man* stop by the desk. She asked the man on the line to hold and then turned to the group of men.

"Hello, Mr. Wilson. There is a Mr. Butler on line two. He says it's urgent."

Liane's boss frowned and nodded. "I'll take it in my office."

He began to walk away and then turned. "Oh, Melanie Rogers, MacAuley Chandler. I believe you already know everyone else. I'll be back in a few minutes."

MacAuley Chandler grinned at Melanie and said, "Take your time, Frank."

"Yeah, Frank, we're finished anyway," added Joe Sparks, the company accountant. He grinned at Melanie and tried to leer at her, but on his boyish face, it didn't quite make it. "There's no one to hear your calls for help, now. You may commence begging for our mercy."

Melanie laughed and shook her head. "Sorry, Joe. I know too many dirty secrets about you guys to be afraid."

Gary Lyons, a computer programmer, grinned and splayed a hand on his chest. "Not me. I have no skeletons."

Regarding him thoughtfully, Melanie pursed her lips. She leaned toward him and whispered something in his ear. Gary suddenly blushed and shifted uncomfortably. He glanced around at the curious stares of his co-workers.

"How did you—never mind. I, uh, I'll be in my office."

He murmured something about witches and walked away.

Joe stepped back and held his hands before him. "I'm not going to ask. I've known you too long." He then pointed to the other two men who remained. "But what about these two? You only just met Mac, and I can't imagine Arnie having any interesting secrets."

Joe hadn't meant the remark to be a slur, but Arnie's pale eyes narrowed in defense of his injured pride. Instead of retaliating, he shrugged and looked back at Melanie.

Her brow crinkling thoughtfully, Melanie considered Arnie Edwards, a marketing vice president. Arnie smiled vaguely at her. She smiled back at him and leaned forward, whispering softly.

Arnie coughed and stepped abruptly away. "I never told—how—who told you that?"

Laughing, Melanie shrugged. "I'm a newspaperman, Arnie. We never reveal our sources."

Joe hooted with laughter. "Newspaperman? Liane probably told you whatever it was. She knows everything that goes on around here."

Arnie laughed along with them, but his expression was cautious as he looked at Melanie. He mumbled something about needing to get to work on a report and dashed off down the corridor.

MacAuley Chandler, reviewing all of this with an enigmatic smile, turned to Melanie. "Are you the keeper of secrets in this town?"

Joe leaned back on the reception desk shaking his head morosely. "Melanie never forgets anything. She can remember things that happened in grade school. Every stupid stunt, every indiscretion, every embarrassing situation, every faux pas. Nothing escaped her. I think she's got it all written down in a little notebook somewhere. She's either planning a massive blackmail attempt, or she's gathering fodder for a gossip column in that rag she works for."

"Rag? I beg your pardon, you illiterate philistine. The *Bayview Herald* is an exemplary local newspaper. But perhaps you would like me to print an account of an incident that occurred some five years ago out at the reservoir on a muggy summer night?"

Joe's mouth dropped open. "Good Lord, what were you doing, hiding in the bushes?"

Not waiting for nor expecting an answer, he shook his finger at her. "If I find out you're psychic, I'm going to be embarrassed in the extreme. And what did you tell poor Edwards and Lyons?"

"I can't tell you that. I wouldn't be the keeper of secrets if I did."

Joe laughed good-naturedly and shrugged. "Well, I don't know about you, Chandler, but I'm beating a hasty retreat before I'm bitterly humiliated in my workplace."

Mac grinned. "Oh, I don't know. I think I'll risk it. I have been known to keep a few secrets myself."

Joe ambled toward his office without noticing Melanie's sheepish expression.

Shrugging innocently, she returned Mac's smile. He was even better looking up close than he had been through her telephoto lens, and she hoped Liane remained in the rest room for at least five more minutes. Until his last words to Joe, she had wondered if MacAuley Chandler remembered her. Gazing up at him, Melanie was trying to decide if his eyes were dark, dark brown or black when he spoke again.

"So, Miss Rogers, we meet at last." He remembered. She was determined to stop the blush that threatened to stain her fair cheeks. She smiled brightly and nodded. She wasn't sure if she should say anything, but was saved when he inquired, "Are you waiting for someone or do you work here?"

The rich smoothness of his baritone voice was having a very positive effect on Melanie's nervous system. So was the lock of dark hair that was threatening to fall on its owner's smooth tanned forehead. And his eyes had to be black, because she couldn't see his pupils.

"Actually," she said smoothly, "I'm waiting for my lunch date."

He was still smiling, but Melanie detected a slight change of mood.

"Really," he said. "Anybody special?"

Melanie felt her pulse increase. It was almost too perfect to be believed, but was he really interested in her? Never having been overly aware of her looks, Melanie didn't consider her big hazel eyes and long auburn hair together with a peaches-and-cream complexion to be particularly beautiful. Attractive, yes, but not beautiful. Especially in these days of short punky haircuts and tanning booths. Mac-Auley Chandler, however, was looking at her as if he thought she was beautiful. Horoscope or not, she was feeling very attracted to this stranger.

"Special?" Melanie repeated softly, and realized that she was flirting with this man. She rarely flirted because she usually felt it was not a very intellectual or honest pastime. But now . . . Settling her hips back on the desk, she nodded. "I would say that it is definitely someone special."

He sighed in mock remorse. "Lucky guy."

She grinned up at him and wondered why he was in town. Men like this just didn't drift into Bayview. She'd never seen a man like him anywhere, and she liked to think of herself as fairly well traveled.

"Do you work here, Mr. Chandler?" She knew he didn't, but he didn't know that.

"Please, call me Mac. Yes and no. I'm a consultant."

Melanie sifted this information and noticed absently that he was wearing a Rolex watch. No wedding ring.

"What do you do at this infamous newspaper, Miss Rogers, or may I call you Melanie?"

Why was it that she felt as if she were hearing her own name for the first time?

"Please do. I write and supply occasional photographs."

"Really? What kind of writing? Perhaps I've read something you've written."

Melanie considered the shape of the cleft in his squared chin and said, "I write features for the entertainment section of the *Herald*."

He seemed to be considering the cleavage revealed by the neckline of the jumpsuit. Melanie felt herself starting to turn red again and attempted to distract him by levering herself to a standing position. But when she placed her hands on the desk to support her weight, they came to rest on a file folder that slipped out from under her, causing her to plop back rather ungracefully onto the desk while the papers in the file fluttered to the floor.

She didn't have to worry about him seeing her turn red now. She looked at the papers on the floor and then looked up at him. To his credit, he didn't say a word. But the humor in his eyes told her he was enjoying himself. He didn't directly mention her little slip. Instead, he picked up right where he was before her inelegant turn.

"Did you go to college for that, or did you just fall into it?"

After taking a few seconds to realize that he was referring to her job, Melanie's hazel eyes narrowed. For the first time since meeting Mac Chandler, Melanie bristled. She had had to put up with a lot of flack before proving herself a competent journalist and reviewer.

"I have a degree in telecommunications and film with a minor in art history, and I have been accepted into several programs to study for my master's degree. But I haven't decided if that is what I want to do yet."

His eyes widened slightly, then he grinned. Perfect white teeth gleamed at her, and Melanie wondered if he had been born with them or if dentists and orthodontia were responsible. She decided that only God could create a smile that beautiful.

"If you don't mind my asking, why aren't you writing for a major-market newspaper?"

Melanie sighed. People would never understand that she loved living in Bayview and that she simply didn't have the driving ambition to slug it out in the rat race to the top. She usually didn't bother to explain to people that she wrote regularly for a Portland daily in addition to her weekly coverage of the county events for Bayview. She preferred to let people find out for themselves that she was a competent and talented journalist. But this was different.

"Let's just say that I like it just fine where I am and that occasionally I sell articles to major newspapers and magazines."

"This person you are meeting for lunch," he said suddenly. "Are you in a serious relationship with him?"

Melanie smiled and wondered why he had assumed that her lunch date was with a man and why she had let him assume it.

"It isn't that kind of a relationship, Mac."

His lips curled upward, and he glanced toward Frank Wilson's office door.

"Well, then, would you like to have dinner with me tomorrow night?"

Melanie feigned a dramatic expression of consideration and then said, "I believe I would enjoy that very much."

"Great," he said warmly. "I'll let you pick the restaurant since it's your town. How's seven?"

"Fine." Melanie turned and wrote her address on a slip of paper and handed it to him. He had just slipped it into his pocket when Liane's head appeared around the corner. With her was Jackie Turner, the executive receptionist. Everyone in town would know about this by five o'clock, and she and

Mac hadn't even had a date yet! Melanie knew that her sister had been waiting and watching because of the smirk on her face.

Melanie pushed herself off the desk and noticed that the top of her head just came to Mac's nose. And she was wearing three-inch heels. Even though at five foot four she was far from tall, she wasn't exactly short, either. Tall, dark and handsome. This was beginning to feel like a dream. She was suddenly hoping that this wasn't a bad joke planned by the gods.

"Ready, Liane?"

Liane smiled and nodded. "I see you've met Mr. Chandler."

"Yes," Melanie agreed, noting the slightly surprised but satisfied look on his face. "Liane is my big sister, Mac. Even though she used to bully me around, I still think she's special."

She waved at him as they got on the elevator, and she laughed, as did Mac, at the confused expression on Liane's face and at the equally confused expression on Jackie's face as she picked up the file and its contents from the floor.

During lunch, Melanie pumped information about Mac from Liane.

"You know, Mel, I don't think I have ever seen you so interested in a man. Mom always said you were too picky, and every year on your birthday most of the family sighs and declares that you are an intellectual snob who will likely die a spinster."

"Oh, please, Liane, spare me. Just because you got married right out of college and have your two kids and your two cars and your yuppie trappings, don't presume it's what I want."

Liane laughed; this was a regular topic.

"All I'm saying is that I'm glad to see that our hormones are not defective."

"My hormones are fine, Liane. Now, tell me what you know about Mac."

"Mac," her sister said, "is a consultant from Salem who is here to evaluate the programming department."

Melanie munched on a tomato from her chef's salad and asked, "What else?"

Liane frowned. "What do you mean?"

"What else do you know about him?"

"You really are interested, aren't you?"

Melanie pushed a cucumber slice with her fork and slowly answered. "I'm not sure, totally, Liane, but, yes, I think I'm very interested. I'll have to wait until after our dinner date tomorrow before I say anything else."

"I knew it," her sister breathed. "The minute I saw him, I thought that here, finally, was someone you wouldn't turn up your persnickety nose at."

"Really?"

Liane grinned. "I was going to ask him to dinner next week, but now it looks as if I won't have to. But I do think you should go slow. You don't go out much, and, well, it can be dangerous to fall for good looks. And I can't remember you ever being so interested in any man."

Melanie put down her fork and looked at her sister. "I haven't as far as I can remember, either. It's just... well...I'm not sure I can explain it, Liane."

Liane smiled. "Chemistry."

"Hmm?"

"A chemical reaction. Some of the less couth people call it lust."

Melanie laughed. "Maybe. Then again, who knows? You said he was from Salem. What else can you tell me?"

"Oh," her sister answered, "nothing. Only that he is being drooled over by every woman at WilCom. Except me, naturally."

"Naturally. Chuck would hardly stand for drool stains on your clothes when you come home, and what would your children think?"

Liane laughed and then reached for her purse.

"Speaking of my children, you promised to referee the swim meet Saturday. Poor old Mr. O'Brien is still in the hospital. Here's the starter's pistol. Chuck asked me to get it from the shop. For some reason, it was only going off every other time."

As Liane gave the pistol to her, Melanie darted a quick look around the restaurant, smiling weakly.

"Liane, why didn't you wait until we got outside? Now everyone in here thinks we are homicidal maniacs."

Liane waved at the two elderly ladies at the next table.

"Hello, Mrs. Horton, Mrs. Atherton." Then she turned back to her sister. "No they don't. They know my husband is the swim coach. Besides, they've known us practically all our lives. Be careful, though, there are blanks in it."

Melanie sighed. Liane was supposed to be the logical one. "Why are there . . . never mind."

She put the pistol in her purse and hoped she wasn't stopped by the highway patrol. She would have a fun time trying to explain why she had a gun in her possession.

"What are you doing this afternoon?" Liane asked as the waiter took her credit card.

"First I am going to run some errands. Then I have to drop off some film reviews I wrote for the paper and watch the video of the one I'm reviewing next."

"What are you working on for next week's column?"

"I'm doing a photo essay on the old Strand Theater that the historical society is trying to get restored. In fact, I'm going to finish taking the pictures this afternoon when I finish my errands.''

Liane smiled. ''Good, I like that old place. Chuck and I spent many an evening during high school necking in that theater.''

''Liane!'' Melanie laughed. ''What would Mom say?''

''Probably that she and Dad spent many an evening during high school necking in that theater.''

Melanie was still grinning over her sister's last words and wondering if she should use them in her story as she parked her slightly aged but still running hatchback on the street across from the park, right behind a sleek black Jaguar. He was back. What was it about the town square that was so appealing to Mac Chandler? She looked over at the newsstand and then noticed that Mac was talking on the phone in the open booth next to it, his back to her. Why was she using a public phone when he probably had an office at his disposal at WilCom?

Melanie pulled her camera bag out of her car as she contemplated his motives. Maybe he would tell her if she asked him over dinner tomorrow. Then again, maybe he would want to know how she knew he had been there.

Deciding she was better off not knowing, she checked her filters and film and then strolled over to the park. It was a beautiful June afternoon, and the Oregon coast was breathtaking in the distance. Melanie took a few minutes to walk across the park to take in the beauty of the ocean. She inhaled deeply of the fresh salt air before turning away to walk back through the park. There were children playing, some young people throwing a Frisbee and several couples having picnic lunches on the sun-warmed grass. She waved to a few people she knew and to some younger friends, children of friends, who had known her all their lives.

She walked along the edge of the park to a bench that was directly across from the Strand Theater. It was a beautiful old building that had been built in 1924 at the height of the silent-movie era. Over the years it had fallen on hard times, and the owners had not had the money required to keep it in repair. The local historical society was trying to gain public support to declare the building a landmark and restore it, but the going was slow. Melanie had decided to do a photo feature on the history of the building and on the present movement to save it.

After taking several pictures with her wide-angle lens, Melanie switched to her telephoto lens to get closeups of the details of the ornamentation, which was decaying more every year. She clicked away, marveling at the craftsmanship. She thought it was a shame that the glass-and-steel era of functionalism and cost effectiveness had taken the place of the beauty of sculpted concrete and carved wood.

Melanie was a romanticist and an idealist, and she rarely bothered to keep her feelings about anything to herself. She was active in several organizations to preserve the environment, save the whales, stop nuclear-waste dumping and, now, preserve local landmarks. She was known around town as the protector of the underdogs of society, and Melanie secretly liked the description. It made her feel good to help worthy organizations.

As she was about to take the telephoto lens off her camera, Melanie saw Mac Chandler step away from the telephone booth. She raised the camera to her eye and clicked off several pictures of Mac as he walked along the street toward his car. She felt like a private detective on a television show. She imagined he was quite photogenic. His high cheekbones and the angles and lines of his face suggested a person who photographed well. She was looking forward to their date the next evening and was mentally going through her wardrobe when a sudden movement caught her eye.

Just as Mac reached the curb and stepped into the street to walk around his car to the driver's side, another car stopped beside him. At first Melanie thought it was someone who wanted his parking spot, but then the car door opened and a man jumped out and shoved Mac into the back seat. She almost dropped the camera, but then managed to click off several pictures of the man who was obviously kidnapping Mac.

Melanie realized that she should do something, but for a moment couldn't decide what. Her mind was frozen, and she could not even breathe. Then, as she watched the car drive off, she shoved her camera into its bag and raced for her own car, pulling her car keys out of her pocket as she ran. Jerking the door open, she leaped in and jammed the key into the ignition. The car's tires squealed pulling away from the curb, attracting the attention of several passersby. She turned right, the direction she had seen the car turn. It was a dark brown, late model car, and Melanie wasn't sure of the make.

She drove along the local road for more than ten minutes before she spotted the car. It was not speeding, but calmly rolling toward the coast highway. Melanie frantically tried to remember all the detective and police shows she had seen and hoped she was doing the right things so that they wouldn't know they were being followed.

As the minutes passed, Melanie began to wonder where they were going. She could easily keep them in sight and stay a quarter of a mile back. The motion of the car had a calming effect on her hammering pulse, and she tried to figure out what was happening.

Who were the men who had grabbed Mac? Why had they grabbed him? Were they kidnappers? Maybe Mac's family was wealthy and he was going to be held for ransom. Or maybe Mac was a criminal, too. Melanie placed that unpleasant thought as far into the recesses of her scattered mind as possible. He couldn't be a criminal. His eyes were too honest. Melanie was a true believer that the eyes were the windows to the soul, and MacAuley Chandler's eyes were not those of a criminal.

She knew she should have gone immediately to the police, but then they would have gotten away. Now she knew why people had car phones. She hadn't even gotten close enough to get the license-plate number. But she doubted it would do much good; the car was probably stolen.

Having been the one and only reviewer of movies and television for the *Bayview Herald* had exposed Melanie to more than her fair share of television police and detective shows. She had learned a lot about criminal-justice procedures and about the ways and means of detective work. Her first priority was to see that Mac was all right. If she saw him get out of the car with the men and that he was not in any immediate danger, she would then find the nearest telephone booth and call the authorities.

After driving along the coast for a bit more than half an hour, she realized that they were just outside the city of Lansport, thirty miles south of Bayview. The car pulled off onto a deserted scenic overlook. Melanie slowed her car and pulled off the road several hundred feet away. She got out her camera and looked through the telephoto lens.

She saw the man who had grabbed Mac get out of the back seat and drag Mac with him. Another man got out from behind the wheel and joined them. Mac's hands had been tied behind his back, he was wearing a blindfold, and one of the men had a gun. The men dragged Mac to the edge of the cliff. One man took off Mac's blindfold and then waved his hand out at the ocean and then pointed down. Melanie thought that it didn't take a genius to figure out what they were threatening. Then the other man asked Mac something. He stood stiffly before them, his stance indicating his refusal to cooperate.

Melanie wished she could hear what they were saying.
Again, she wished she had a car phone to call the police. She
wished she could remember what Cagney and Lacey would
do. With a grimace she realized that Cagney and Lacey
would have had backups. Why hadn't she had the brains to
go for the police? This was one time her impulsive nature
might prove detrimental to someone.

Her prayers that nothing violent would happen went un-
answered as she saw one of them thrust his hand into a
pocket then pull it out again. After flexing his fingers, the
man pulled his fist back, aiming it at Mac's jaw.

Mac tried to duck away, but the man's fist glanced off his
forehead near the temple. Melanie blanched as she saw
Mac's big body sag as he lost consciousness. What had he
been hit with? She let out the breath she had been holding
when she saw that the man didn't dump his body over the
cliff.

She was hoping that the men would just go away so she
could go to help Mac, but that was not to be. They argued
for a minute, the man with the gun waving it in Mac's
direction, the other man shaking his head and rubbing his
knuckles. Melanie saw sunlight glinting off his fist. Brass
knuckles.

Her jaw set, she heaped scathing curses on the head of the
man who had hit Mac. Then she saw Mac move, and the
men bent down to drag him up, propping him upright
against the one who held the gun, which rested menacingly
against Mac's throat.

Mac was shaking his head. The man who had hit him
suddenly drew back his arm and crashed his fist into Mac's
stomach.

Chapter Two

No!'' Melanie was screaming even as she slammed her little car into drive and peeled out toward the men, blaring her horn. If she could just distract them, maybe she could stop them from beating Mac to death. Or from shooting him. If only she had a—

She pulled her purse onto her lap as she watched the man with the gun jerk his head up at the sound of the approaching car. He hid his gun behind his back, stepping away from Mac, who then fell to his knees. Melanie realized that they wouldn't want any witnesses to what they were trying to do. Her hands were shaking and her mind was threatening to numb. She forced herself to concentrate.

Her mind racing as she scrambled inside the car, Melanie stayed on the edge of the road and left the engine running as she threw the car into park. She then pulled the starter's pistol from her purse and prayed it looked real. The day was cloudy, but it was still hours before sunset, and everything she did would be visible to these men.

She jumped out of the car and pointed the gun at Mac's would-be assailant, bracing her forearms on the roof of the car. He was pointing his gun at her by now, and she swallowed nervously, trying to appear calm.

"Drop it or you're a dead man," she yelled. Oh, God, what a stupid thing to say. "I have a clear shot, buddy, you'd have to shoot through the car, what's it gonna be?"

She hoped that these criminals hadn't watched the rerun of *Police Story* on television the night before, because she was stealing her dialogue. The man holding the gun glanced toward his companion and then shrugged and dropped his gun, his hands rising and a sardonic expression lifting his eyebrows.

"Good thinking," Melanie said, glad that they couldn't see her legs shaking. "Now, untie him and put him in my car."

The two men looked at each other and then at Melanie.

"What are you, a cop?" the first man asked.

"What do you care? I've got the gun. Oh, and kick yours over here," she added as an afterthought.

The man looked as if he was going to grab the gun, so Melanie squeezed the trigger on the starter pistol and a blank went off. It sounded real to her, and it must have had the same effect on the two men because they were sprawled on the ground when Melanie opened her eyes. She gritted her teeth to stop them chattering. Then she took a deep breath. Making an effort to keep her voice low and slow she said, "Now that I have your attention, kick the gun over here."

Both men stood up, and the first man kicked the gun over to the side of the road. Melanie stepped to the end of the car and sank on her knees to retrieve it, never taking her eyes off the two men. She had seen too many bad TV detectives lose their lives because they looked away for a second. She rose again, holding the real gun in her left hand, and the starter's pistol in her right hand. She waved both guns at the men.

"Now, put him in my car, and don't try anything. I might get a little jumpy, and one of these might go off."

She watched as the two men struggled with the unconscious weight of Mac's body. She decided to try to memorize them so she could identify them later.

It was then that she realized they were nondescript men. Both were around six feet tall, plain brown hair, average features. With a chill she knew that they were nondescript for a reason. Professional thugs. In Bayview, Oregon? Maybe they were semiprofessional.

As they slammed the car door, she glanced at the brown car. "Throw me your car keys," she said.

The two men looked nervously at each other and Melanie pointed the real gun in their direction.

"You," she said to the first man. "Go over and get the keys."

The man walked over and began rummaging around the front seat. Did they have another gun? Melanie fired another blank. The keys came sailing toward her, landing just a few inches from her feet. She then dropped the starter's pistol onto the floorboard and picked up the keys, flinging them onto her back seat.

"Listen, lady, you may have gotten lucky this time, but you can tell your boyfriend when he wakes up that if he wants to avoid any more unfortunate accidents, he'd better give it back."

Melanie forced her face not to show confusion and surprise. What was he talking about? She knew little about Mac, but even less about these men. She knew instinctively that if Mac did have whatever they were referring to, that he had a good reason to have it. She wasn't very good at poker, but she decided to try to bluff them.

"I don't think you are in a position to make many threats, creep," she taunted. "I think I might just encourage him to keep it."

She had no idea what "it" was, but it got a reaction out of the two men. They shifted nervously and glanced at each other and at her. Melanie wondered why they would be nervous, then her eyes widened. They were working for someone else, of course. The fact that they had botched this job probably wouldn't earn them any Brownie points.

The second man spoke this time. "I don't think you would do something that stupid."

Now that she knew that they had something or someone to fear, Melanie was feeling braver. "Stupid? I don't think so. It could be that Mr. Chandler has just decided to do business elsewhere."

The first man took a step forward, but stopped when Melanie pointed the real gun at him. He growled in frustration. "Maybe *you* are stupid, lady. If he tries to sell that information to anyone else, he would end up with more than just a bump on his head."

Melanie shuddered and decided that she had had enough of this strange conversation. She didn't understand what was going on, and her arm hurt from holding the gun.

"Get in the car," she said.

The two men walked slowly to their car, one on either side. They each opened a back door and got in.

When the second door had shut, Melanie jumped into her car, dropped the real gun on the floorboard, shifted into drive and shot off down the highway. Glancing over at Mac, she saw a trickle of blood above his left temple and realized that she would have to get him to a hospital. She also knew that those men were probably hot wiring their car and coming after her. The only advantage she had was that she knew the town because her best friend from high school, Nancy Doyle, lived in Lansport now.

Upon reaching the city limits and still not seeing the brown car, Melanie nevertheless drove in aimless patterns through the streets until she was sure no one was following. Mac had been semiconscious when the men had dumped him into her car, and now he was beginning to groan. She pulled into the driveway of a small bungalow in a quiet neighborhood and threw the car into Park.

Leaving Mac in the car, Melanie raced to the front door, knocking and opening the front door at the same time. A beautiful brunette was sitting on her sofa, watching television. She was startled at the intrusion, but not surprised.

"Mel, what is it?"

"I'm sorry, Nancy, but I really need a favor."

Nancy was on her feet and nodding as Melanie stepped back onto the small front porch. Her friend was right behind her, stopping just long enough to grab her purse and lock the door. She caught up with Melanie as she opened the car door.

Peering into the car, Nancy's blue eyes widened. "What happened to him? Who is he?"

Melanie held the front seat back forward as Nancy climbed into the back seat, stepping on the starter pistol then sitting on the car keys.

As Melanie backed out of the driveway, Nancy murmured, "This is gonna be a doozy, isn't it?"

Breathing a ragged sigh, Melanie began to tell her friend of the day's events. She kept it brief and was done as she cautiously pulled into the parking lot of a small medical clinic.

She came around to the passenger's side of the car and helped Mac out. He was groggy and incoherent, but he could stand. With Nancy's help, they got to the door. Melanie then turned to her friend.

"Would you please take my car and hide it nearby? It's like a beacon. Then walk back here. Hopefully, they'll check the county hospital first. Maybe this won't be serious and we'll be gone before they realize this place exists.

Nancy nodded, taking Melanie's keys. "Sure, Mel. I know just the place."

With that, Nancy was gone, and Melanie turned to open the door and help a groggy Mac through it.

When they entered the building, a nurse rushed over. "What happened?" the nurse asked, helping Melanie lead Mac into an examining room.

Melanie had wondered what she was going to say in answer to that particular question.

"He got in a fight and fell down."

The nurse just nodded, jotting down the information. "Has your husband ever been a patient here before?"

Her husband?

"Uh, no, he hasn't. We're new in town."

Melanie decided it was best that the nurse and doctor didn't know either of them. That way neither of them could tell anything useful to anyone who might ask.

When the nurse left the room to get the doctor and the paperwork, Melanie went through Mac's pockets in search of identification and other personal papers. She jammed everything into her purse after checking his driver's license and other papers to see if anything mentioned allergies or prescriptions. The only thing she found out was that he was allergic to penicillin.

When the nurse, accompanied by a doctor, returned a few minutes later, Melanie was led outside to the waiting room. She'd given their names as Mr. and Mrs. Nicholas Charles and hoped neither the doctor nor the nurse were fans of *The Thin Man*.

When she had filled out the forms for the nurse, duly recording MacAuley Chandler's allergy, she carried them over to the desk. She wanted to see Mac. She had to make sure that he didn't blab his real name to the doctor. She wanted to leave no trace of who they really were. She had made up a phony address and telephone number to accompany the phony names. As she sat staring at an unbelievably bad reproduction of a Rembrandt still life, she found herself wondering if she were incredibly brilliant or just incredibly stupid.

She had decided upon the latter when the movement of the outside door caught her eye.

Nancy had returned. Melanie smiled at her in spite of the circumstances. Nancy was so unbelievably calm. Nothing shook her up. Nothing embarrassed her. Melanie had known Nancy ever since the fifth grade, and she didn't think she had ever seen her friend rattled.

That was Melanie's domain. They had had many escapades and misadventures in school, and it was always Nancy who stayed calm and never flinched in the face of punishment. Melanie had always admired her quick mind and serene attitude.

Even now, after she had been dragged through the streets of Lansport with a semiconscious man and a frazzled best friend, Nancy looked calm and in control.

"Well?"

"I don't know," Melanie said. "He's in there. I gave fake names and all that."

"Mmm. You wouldn't want them to trace you."

Melanie nodded, then shook her head.

"Criminy. What am I doing? What have I done? I should have called the police."

Nancy nodded thoughtfully. "Why haven't you?"

"Because there wasn't time. I had to follow them. And then I drove around some to make sure I had lost them. Then I went straight to your house."

"Why don't you call now?" Nancy gestured toward the pay phone on the wall.

Melanie considered it. She also considered what the men on the overlook had said. "I think I'll wait until I find out how he is. Maybe he'd rather call them himself. He certainly knows more about this than I do."

"All right." Nancy knew something was off center, but she also knew that Melanie was nervous about something other than Mac's condition and that she would tell her friend about it when she wanted to and not before.

Glancing around the outer office, Melanie asked, "Do you know anyone who works here?"

Her question was abrupt, but didn't phase the placid Nancy. "I don't think so, but, just in case..."

She rose gracefully and went to the pay phone, standing with her back to the front desk. Melanie smiled gratefully at her. Nancy winked and returned her smile.

Melanie's hands were clenched in her lap, and as she willed her fingers to relax, she moaned. Nancy turned to look at her. Pointing to her bare ring finger, Melanie mouthed, "They think we're married." Nancy rolled her eyes and pulled a ring off her own finger, shoving it onto Melanie's finger and twisting it around so that it looked like a thin gold band.

Her thoughts returned to Mac as she looked up at the swinging door leading to the examining rooms. She saw the door open and was on her feet.

"How is he?" she asked the nurse, glancing nervously at the front door of the clinic. She kept expecting the two thugs to come bursting through the door, shooting everything and everyone in sight. Logic didn't mean much to her petrified mind.

"I'm sure he'll be fine, Mrs. Charles," the nurse said. "The fact that he's conscious is a good sign."

Melanie's head jerked up. "I have to see him."

She started toward the examining room, but was stopped when the doctor opened the door and stood facing her. His expression was clouded.

"What is it? Is he going to be all right?"

The doctor smiled and put out his hand. As Melanie shook it, he said, "I'm Dr. Burton, Mrs. Charles. Don't worry, he's going to be fine. But there is a problem."

Melanie couldn't believe it. What now?

"What's wrong, Doctor?"

"Well, the blow to his head has caused him an uncertain amount of memory loss. I'm sure it's only temporary and his memory will be fully restored when the swelling goes down."

Melanie's head was swimming. Amnesia? This was turning into a nightmare. The doctor was still talking, and she had to concentrate to understand him.

"I've taken X rays, but I don't think he has a concussion. If he does, he'll have to go to the hospital. Just a minute, I'll go and check."

As the doctor disappeared into a room down the hall, Melanie slipped into the room where Mac was. He was sitting up, a bandage on his head and a confused look on his face. He looked at Melanie and appeared to have trouble focusing.

"Mac?" She asked tentatively. "How do you feel?"

"Like I got run over by a beer truck. The doctor said my memory would return later, but right now...I'm sorry, do I know you?"

Melanie didn't know what to say. Her mind flew over the events of the afternoon. It seemed inconceivable that they had just met six hours before. While she was searching for something to say, the doctor walked into the room with an X ray.

"Well, good news, folks. Mr. Charles, you do not have a concussion, but I do recommend that you go home and let your lovely wife put you to bed and take care of you for several days until the swelling goes down and your memory returns. I've written a prescription for some medication to ease the headaches you'll probably be having. You can have it filled at the clinic pharmacy."

Melanie saw the confused thoughts running across Mac's face as he looked from her to the doctor, and she decided to just get him out of there before their "friends" from the overlook showed up. She could explain later.

"Thank you, Doctor, we appreciate all you've done. Is there anything special I should do to help him regain his memory?"

The doctor shook his head. "No, just continue with your normal routine as much as possible, and it'll come back to him. If it hasn't returned in a few days, take him to see your family doctor. Or bring him back here. Or to a hospital."

Melanie nodded and went over to Mac, who was standing a little shakily beside the examining table. Normal routine? Forget it. There was no way he could go about a normal routine. She had no idea what that was.

"Let's go home, darling," she said, feeling like an accomplice in the crime instead of the rescuer. "You'll be fine."

Out in the lobby, as she deposited Mac in a seat and handed the prescription to the pharmacist, she noticed Nancy slipping quietly outside.

After the prescription was filled, Melanie paid the clinic bill with all the cash she had on her plus some of the cash from Mac's wallet. She then helped him outside. Nancy was waiting just outside the front of the door. They both helped a confused Mac into the car, and Melanie drove off, looking around for signs of the dark brown sedan. Seeing nothing suspicious, she felt a bit more confident.

Until she heard the muffled laughter coming from the back seat.

"What is so amusing?"

Nancy leaned forward between the bucket seats. "Mr. and Mrs. Charles?" She was whispering in Melanie's ear, so that Mac couldn't hear. "I mean, how original. At least you didn't use Smith."

"I'm sorry, it was the best I could do under the circumstances. My mind is mush right now, you know."

Then Melanie laughed. It was outrageous, and she was amazed that neither the doctor nor the nurse had caught on. "I don't believe I couldn't think of anything else." She returned the ring Nancy had loaned her, not noticing Mac's curious eyes following her motions. "This is your fault, Nancy Doyle."

"I beg your pardon?"

Melanie glanced in the rearview mirror at Nancy's grin. "You and your *Thin Man* film festival last week."

"Are you a friend of the family?"

Mac's quiet question brought a new wave of suppressed laughter from Melanie. Nancy turned a perfectly straight face toward him.

"Yes, I am. My name is Nancy Doyle. I've known Melanie for years and years."

"Then we know each other, too?"

Melanie's eyes were huge in her pale face. She held her breath, waiting for Nancy to reply.

"Oh, sure," her friend said smoothly. "I've known you since the beginning of your...relationship. You followed her around, mooning at her until she finally broke down and went out with you."

Melanie patted Mac's hand. "Never mind, Mac, Nancy's just teasing us. She's a real joker." It was her own fault for blabbing about the handsome stranger she'd seen around Bayview.

Backtracking and going around in circles had made the five-minute trip to Nancy's last three times as long. But

Melanie wasn't taking any chances that they had been spotted.

Pulling onto Nancy's street, she surveyed the area one last time before stopping in front of the house. Turning in her seat, she looked into Nancy's intelligent blue eyes.

"Could I park my car in your garage?"

Nancy needed no explanation. A red Escort wouldn't be hard to spot. She nodded, and Melanie let her out of the car. She watched as Nancy opened her garage door and got into her white Mazda. Mac cleared his throat, and Melanie turned abruptly to see him watching her uncertainly.

"Uh, this is going to sound weird, but..."

"Yes?" she prompted gently.

"What is your name?"

Well, that was easy enough. "Melanie."

"That doctor said that we are married."

"Did he?" Melanie was watching Nancy pull out of her garage and onto the street. She heard Mac sigh in frustration and realized that he had said something and she hadn't heard it. "I'm sorry. What was that?"

"I asked why we aren't wearing wedding rings."

Melanie tightened her grip on the steering wheel. She eased her car up the drive and into Nancy's garage. After putting it in park and turning off the engine, she looked over at Mac.

"I'll explain everything, I promise. Why don't we go inside now?"

They got out, and Melanie gathered up the various items littering her car. She dumped the guns and car keys into her bulging purse and went around to see if Mac needed any help. He was woozy, but under his own steam.

Nancy reparked her car in her driveway in front of the garage. Melanie closed the garage door behind her and Mac, and Nancy locked it. Then they all proceeded into the house.

Dropping her purse on the floor, Melanie took Mac's arm and steered him toward the sofa. Nancy locked the door and turned toward the kitchen.

"I think I'll make some tea. Wouldn't that be nice?"

Melanie nodded absently. Mac was looking around at the unfamiliar surroundings apprehensively. Then he looked at her with the same expression.

"I know," she muttered. "I'll try to explain, really I will. If I just figure out where to start."

"What happened to me?" he asked.

She sighed and sat down on the sofa next to him. "You were attacked by two men. One of them hit you with what I think were brass knuckles. That's what caused your head injury. They also hit you in the stomach."

His brow furrowed as he attempted to concentrate on her words. "I don't understand. How do you know about this? Were you with me? Are we married?"

"No, we aren't. The nurse assumed we were, and I figured it would cause less trouble not to set them straight."

It took his battered brain a few minutes to sift through that information. "Trouble?"

Battered brain or no, it hadn't taken him long to go right to the root of the situation. Trouble with a capital *T* and that rhymed with *G* and that stood for guns. Big guys with big guns. She was losing what was left of her mind, she decided.

"You said it, Mac. Trouble."

"What kind of trouble?"

She sighed wearily. "I have no idea, but those guys who knocked you over the head wanted something. And until you can remember what it was, we had better keep out of their way." She chewed on her bottom lip and wondered what she was going to do. Mac sighed and leaned back against the sofa cushions. Melanie suddenly felt guilty. He was in pain, and talking about this probably wasn't good for him right now.

"How do you feel?" What an inane thing to say.

"You don't want to know," he replied. Then he sat up straight. "Someone hit me with brass knuckles? Why?"

"That—" she sighed "—is the $64,000 question."

"How about a hint?"

Melanie rubbed her tense neck. She looked over at Mac, who was patiently waiting for her to explain away the whole mess. She didn't know how to do that. If she couldn't find explanations for herself, how was she supposed to satisfy his curiosity? She shrugged and shook her head.

"I honestly don't know, Mac. You are the only one who knows the answer to that one, and, apparently, your brain isn't issuing any statements at this time."

Even if her words weren't any help, at least he seemed to accept that she was honestly ignorant of the facts. After all, what could he compare them to?

Nancy returned, bearing a tray with cups and saucers and a silver tea service.

"I made herb tea instead. I didn't think that Mac should have caffeine."

Melanie nodded. Mac was rubbing his head, and didn't look as if he would remember anything tonight. Melanie took his bottle of medicine out of her purse, and Nancy poured him some tea.

Rising, Nancy walked toward the hallway that led to two bedrooms and a bathroom. "Mel, I don't think you should take him back to Bayview tonight. I'll make up the guest room for him."

Melanie frowned, then nodded. "You're right, he shouldn't move around any more than necessary."

She turned her attention to the bottle of pills. After struggling with the child-proof cap for a minute, she achieved victory. She shook one out and held it out for him.

"Here, take this. The doctor said it would help the head-aches."

Mac took the pill from her but didn't put it in his mouth. "I want to talk."

"Uh, I don't think that is such a great idea right now. I think you should take that pill and go to bed. We'll talk after you've had some rest."

Mac looked deep into her big hazel eyes and said, "You know, you really are very lovely."

Melanie blushed and wished the man was in his right mind.

"Well, thank you. Now, will you take the pill?"

Mac smiled but didn't take the pill. "Why were there two guns in the car?"

Melanie closed her eyes. This was not easy. "Look, all of this is very complicated and has a great deal to do with things that you obviously can't remember and other things that I have no knowledge of. So I think that the best thing right now is for you to take that pill and go to sleep."

"Do you always bully me when I'm sick?"

Melanie opened her mouth to tell him that she had never seen him sick, but just then, Mac sighed and rubbed tiredly at his eyes. She didn't see any reason not to let him get a good night's sleep before burdening him with information he wouldn't even know what to do about.

She needed time to figure out what to do. That's what she needed, a plan. And Melanie didn't doubt that she could come up with something. Nancy was here, and together the two of them could do anything. Besides, she had spent a great deal of her working hours watching the plots of movies and television shows that attempted to deal with just such situations. Unfortunately, right now, she couldn't remember even one of them. What had Mac asked her? Did she bully him?

"Yes, I do," she finally said. He just smiled and took the pill. She smiled back at him. "Now, come on, you are going to bed."

She showed him where the bathroom was and waited until he came out. Then she showed him where the guest room was. Nancy was just turning down the covers. She smiled serenely at them and left.

Melanie's eyes followed Nancy, then swung back to look at Mac, who was pulling off his shirt. She swallowed at the sight of his broad tanned chest covered with curling dark hair. He was beautiful. And sexy. And... Melanie knew she should leave, but she wanted to stay.

He sat on the bed and sighed. "Whoo, those pills are powerful."

Mac stretched out on top of the bed and was asleep before Melanie could worry about leaving or staying. She looked at his unconscious body and murmured a prayer of thanks that he wasn't still lying on that overlook.

She debated with herself only for a few seconds before going over and pulling off his shoes and socks. Then she unbuckled his belt and pulled it off.

"Great, Mel. The first time you ever undress a man, and he's unconscious."

Melanie felt herself longing to run her hands over his chest, but told herself she would rather do it when he was awake. She then unzipped his pants and pulled them off as quickly as she could, and then got him under the covers. He was sleeping so deeply that he never knew what happened. Melanie couldn't resist brushing his hair back with her fingers and kissing his forehead. They had been through so much today, and he couldn't even remember most of it.

"When we tell our grandchildren about this, Mac, we'll laugh. I hope."

The softly spoken statement took Melanie by surprise. She frowned at the figure on the bed and wondered at the influence he had wrought over her life in just the few hours since she had met him. But she wasn't uncomfortable with that influence. That was what had surprised her. It felt right. And she knew at that moment that when she had least expected it, the man she had been waiting for had stormed into her life.

And he didn't know who he was.

Chapter Three

Melanie shut the door to the guest bedroom and walked slowly back into the living room, absently twirling a strand of auburn hair. She sat on the sofa and suppressed a cry of frustration. Then she glanced at Nancy, who sat cross-legged on the floor, next to the coffee table.

"We have to do something, Nancy. We have to help him. We have to call the police. They're going to want to know who those men were and why they attacked Mac. What do we tell them?" Her barrage ceased as she drew a breath and her hazel eyes widened. "What if he turns out to be one of them? They did say that he had stolen something from them. Or at least they implied it. What if we're harboring a criminal in your bedroom?"

"Mel," Nancy said, laughing. "You may have to watch television and movies to review them, but you don't have to start thinking like them."

Melanie nodded absently. "You're right. But, really, we do have to do something." Her eyes fell on her purse, laying on the floor next to the door where she had dropped it. In it were all the personal effects Mac had been carrying when she had taken him to the clinic. She knew she shouldn't, but she retrieved the purse and dumped its contents onto the glass top of the table.

Nancy watched her friend's movements with a wary blue gaze. When she saw the man's wallet, she smiled. "Good thinking, Mel."

After separating her own belongings and returning them to her purse, Melanie and Nancy began to learn a few things about MacAuley Chandler.

Melanie began with his wallet. She started to pull out the items, placing them on the tabletop. Pausing, she looked at Nancy. "You don't think he'll be mad at us for invading his privacy, do you?"

Nancy laughed. "You saved his life, and I gave him a place to stay. He'd better be grateful."

Melanie nodded. She picked up the first item. "Driver's license. Oregon. Wendell MacAuley Chandler."

"Wendell?" Nancy said softly.

Melanie's lips curved slightly. "I would bet a large sum of money that very few people are privy to that particular bit of information." Then she continued reading the information. "He lives in Salem. Born March 7."

"A Pisces. You're also a water sign. That's good," Nancy offered.

Melanie rolled her eyes and refused to comment. "Thirty-one years old. He checked the organ-donor box. Blood type AB."

Placing the license on the table, she pulled out several business cards with the name of Chandler Enterprises on it. Mac's name was in a corner. An address in Salem and a telephone number were in the other.

Melanie made sure to return each item to the place she had found it after Nancy had looked at them. Also in the wallet were two pictures, one was of a middle-aged couple, and the other was a graduation picture of a young man who looked a little like Mac. Melanie extracted the pictures from their plastic coverings and flipped them over to check for any names or dates. The first picture had a few words scrawled on the back. "Mom and Dad, 1982."

She handed Nancy the picture. Nancy's dark head bent over it for a few seconds. "Mac looks just like his father, except that his eyes are like his mother's."

On the reverse of the second picture was an inscription. Melanie read it aloud. " 'To Mac, the best brother in the world. Now that I'm an adult, will you let me drive your Jag? Love, Kyle.' " The date on the picture was ten years ago.

Nancy smiled at the words and at the picture. "Not exactly a homely family."

They both laughed. Melanie was glad Nancy was there. Her friend was managing to diffuse the tension that had been building in Melanie all afternoon and into evening.

The next item was the medical information card that stated Mac's allergy to penicillin. There were several credit cards and insurance cards. Obviously he was a man who was at least secure, if not well off—the credit cards were all gold cards. He had been carrying $273.65 in cash. Melanie laughed. "I have about that much money in the bank."

She laid the wallet aside and began examining the remaining two key rings, one with his car keys on it, the other with the key to his hotel room at the Bayview Arms.

"That's it?" Nancy asked.

Melanie nodded. "There's not much to go on. Maybe we should call his business number and see what happens."

"It's after six. You'd probably just get a recording or a service." Nodding absently, Melanie frowned at the array of items they had scrutinized. Her troubled gaze garnered Nancy's attention. "What is it?"

Shrugging, Melanie gestured at the items on the table. "I don't know. It seems like there's something missing."

"Like what?"

"I'm not sure. There should be . . ."

When Melanie's voice trailed off and she stared blankly at the wall behind Nancy, her friend put a hand on Melanie's knee. "Mel?"

Dragging her gaze to meet Nancy's, Melanie took a deep breath. "It may not be relevant, but I gave my address to Mac earlier today. We were going to go to dinner tomorrow night."

Nancy's blue eyes widened. "And it's not here?" When Melanie shook her head, Nancy pulled on a strand of dark brown hair.

"Maybe he went back to his motel and left it there."

Melanie worried a thumbnail with her teeth. "Maybe. But what if that isn't it? What if those men who grabbed him took it?"

Nancy reached for the telephone sitting on an end table. "Then you can't go back to your apartment until we find out what is going on."

"Who are you calling?"

Dialing the phone, Nancy explained. "The police. They're local and they may not know much, but they're all we've got. Besides, I know a few of the guys down there."

Fifteen minutes later, Nancy hung up the telephone. She had explained the facts to an officer she knew, and he had told her that without Mac's ability to identify his attackers, there wasn't much to go on. Melanie was welcome to come look at mug books, but he doubted it would be more than a waste of time. He promised they would investigate the area around the overlook and that they would watch for the car. He told her to call back when Mac's memory returned.

Melanie sighed. "So, that didn't help much."

"No, but we're not done yet. What we should have already done is try to get in touch with his family."

Agreeing sheepishly, Melanie picked up the phone and dialed information for Salem. Not having a first name for his parents, she asked for a number for Kyle Chandler. She was given a number and dialed it. A recorded message asked for her name and number.

"Uh, hello Kyle, you don't know me, but this call is about your brother, Mac. It's important you call as soon as possible."

Giving her name and Nancy's number, she hung up and looked at her friend. "I hate machines. I always feel pressured to perform." Mac had to get his memory back and fast. What had the doctor said? Being in his normal environment and routine would hasten the return of his memory. Melanie sighed. The poor man's psyche was most likely in a state of total confusion.

Staring at the two sets of keys, Melanie wondered if "it" was in either Mac's hotel room or his car. She knew that, for security reasons, the small local hotels only allowed guests or people accompanied by guests of the hotels, upstairs to the rooms. That ruled out looking in his hotel room for now. "Maybe we could find out more from his car," she speculated.

Blue eyes widened in alarm. "Mel, I don't think that you should even think about doing anything like what I'm thinking you're thinking about."

Melanie reached for the phone. "I think we have to act before they do. If they get to his car, they might tear it up looking for information."

"Well, they've had plenty of time, but I doubt that they would do anything stupid, like stealing Mac's car. There are people all over the square during the day. And in Bayview, I would bet that everyone already knows that that black

Jaguar belongs to Mac. No one will bother that car until after the square closes."

Nodding, Melanie spoke as she dialed. "It's already after six. The square closes at seven. It will take half an hour to get to Bayview, and I'll have to make sure..."

She broke off when the cab company dispatcher answered. Nancy gaped at her friend. When Melanie replaced the receiver, Nancy waved a slender hand in her direction.

"I hope you don't think that you're just going to waltz onto the square and take that Jaguar without being seen?"

Melanie looked up and shrugged. "I have to get the car before they do. I hope I'm not already too late. I think that Jaguar is very important to Mac. He's had it for at least ten years."

"Well, I'm glad you've got a good reason for risking your life."

Melanie's jaw was set, and Nancy sighed. "All right, but I'm coming with you."

Shaking her head, Melanie said, "You can't. You've got to stay here in case Kyle calls before I get back. And Mac might wake up."

Nancy looked resigned. "You are a hardheaded woman, Melanie Rogers. I want you to promise me you'll be careful and not to take any unnecessary chances. A car is nice, but not worth getting hurt or killed over."

"Oh, don't worry, I'll be careful. I just want to try to get the car back before they do. There might be something in it that can help us."

It was a few minutes before seven when the cab neared the square. Melanie asked the driver to turn onto a street that ran parallel to one of the streets of the square. The street opposite the one where Mac's car sat. She wanted to scan the area for any signs of the men who had attacked Mac. They might have come back to stake out his car. Melanie asked the man to circle the square. Her driver looked confused.

She handed him ten dollars and promised more if he would do as she asked, swearing that she wasn't doing anything illegal.

There were still a few people on the streets, getting into their cars after closing their shops. Soon the square would be dark and abandoned.

Why did you have to try this, stupid? She asked more deprecating questions of herself as she looked across the street. Then, as she started to scan the corner, movement arrested her gaze. A car was slowly pulling onto the square. Damn. Asking the driver to stop, she chewed her lip, trying to figure out a plan. The two men were on the street perpendicular to the Jaguar, so she couldn't just go up to it and get in. She needed a distraction or something.

Melanie spoke quickly and quietly to the driver, giving him more money when he hesitated. Then she slid over to the right passenger side of the back seat and gripped the door handle as the taxi turned onto the street where the Jaguar was parked.

The summer sun still hadn't set, but the early evening shadows were lengthening, and Melanie hoped that she was up to the plan she had concocted. She had Mac's keys in her shaking fingers as the cab pulled to a stop next to the Jaguar. Sparing only one glance toward the two men who were getting out of the sedan, Melanie quickly jumped out of the cab and fitted the key into the lock of the driver's door and jerked it open.

It was a 1968 classic Jaguar, and it had a stick shift. Melanie had had exactly one lesson driving a standard-shift car. It had been a hilarious outing in an old car that had belonged to Liane's husband. And it had been at least seven years ago.

"Well, if you think a little thing like this is gonna stop me," she said softly, "think again!" She shoved the key into the ignition and turned it. As the engine turned over, she looked up and saw that the men were standing in the middle of the street.

She crossed her fingers and honked the horn once. The cab then began rolling toward the two men in what appeared to be a game of chicken, causing the two men to stumble back toward their car. Melanie shifted into gear and stepped on the gas a little too fast, causing the car to lurch forward, but luckily the engine didn't stall. She pulled out into the street with tires squealing and gears grinding.

She took the corner without stopping at the stop sign—who was going to give her a ticket? The square was deserted, save the two men getting back into their dark brown sedan and a taxi cab that was leaving as quickly as she was. She glanced into the rearview mirror and saw the brown car making a U-turn to follow her. The cab suddenly appeared to stall in the middle of the street, blocking it. Silently thanking the cab driver for being willing to go along with her, Melanie concentrated on making sure the sedan didn't find her and follow her back to Lansport.

She stepped on the gas and sped off down the street, her mind working overtime in trying to ascertain the quickest route to lose these guys. The advantage she had was that she knew all the alleys and back roads and shortcuts in Bayview. The bad part was that whoever those men were, they were good at what they did, and if she made one mistake, they would win.

She turned off into the maze of a new subdivision that had been built a few years back. Although she had hated the uniformity of the houses and the unartistic, boring landscaping at the time, Melanie was now grateful for it.

She had several friends who lived in this area, and she knew where the dead ends and the outlets to the major streets of the town were. She saw the dark car in the rear-view mirror once, upon entering the development, and then she started her weaving and backtracking. Seeing them go down a dead-end street, she turned in the opposite direction and made for the highway, leaving it less than a quarter of a mile later.

She followed side streets to a county road that led to Lansport. Not seeing anyone behind her, she hoped she had lost them. Then she feared that they would know how to follow her because the smell of a burned clutch was rather obvious. She hoped Mac would forgive her.

She felt a headache coming on. The muscles in her neck and shoulders were knotted from tension. She was not normally a worrier. That was Liane's job in the family. Right now, though, Melanie felt the weight of the world on her tired shoulders. She had the acute sensation that everything was up to her. She was the factor everything relied on to go right—or to go wrong.

Forty-five minutes later, when she turned onto Nancy's street, she pulled over and turned off the engine. She stared down the street, seeing nothing suspicious or out of place. But she felt a strange tension from within her own body.

If all her deductions were right, and she had no guarantees that they were, then she had to get Mac out of town. He couldn't stay holed up at Nancy's. Melanie shook her head to clear it of unwanted thoughts. The sky was almost dark, and her brain had been working at a furious pace for hours. She was trying to figure out a sane explanation for an insane situation. Unfortunately, her body wanted sleep.

"Later, Melanie," she told herself as she got out of the Jaguar and walked up to the porch.

Nancy had been watching for her and flung the door open. "Are you all right?"

Shrugging her tense shoulders, Melanie smiled weakly. "Oh, fine. Where can we hide that car?"

Nancy sighed in exasperation. "I hope it's worth all of this."

They parked the car in Nancy's backyard, and took a tarp from her basement to cover it. Using a flashlight, they searched the car before covering it, finding nothing of interest, except a small spiral notebook with some kind of mathematical scribbling on its pages, tucked into the glove compartment. In the trunk was a duffel bag with clothes and shaving gear. A pair of hiking boots were hanging from its strap by their laces. Hardly anything someone could get beat up over. Or killed for.

Once inside the house, they locked all the doors and checked all the windows. Melanie placed the duffel and boots in the guest room. Mac had rolled onto his stomach, his right arm flung out over the sheets. He had also shoved the covers off his tanned body, so that only his calves were covered. Melanie sighed. The only light in the room came through the window via the crescent moon and bathed the room in a faint silvery glow.

She closed the door and went back into the living room to find Nancy sitting on the sofa, poring over the spiral notebook.

"Does it make any sense to you?" she asked, sinking onto the soft cushions.

"No. I think only he'll know what it is. It just looks like math problems."

Melanie nodded, taking the notebook and glancing at it before dropping it into her purse. "Well, he is a computer consultant. It probably has something to do with what he was doing at WilCom."

With an exaggerated sigh, Nancy slouched down in her armchair. "Now that I can stop worrying about you for the night, I think we could both use a drink."

Surprise lighting her hazel eyes, Melanie watched as Nancy rose and went into the kitchen, returning with two glasses of red wine. Accepting one, Melanie waited until Nancy was once again slouched in the chair.

"Where have you been hiding this? I thought you didn't drink?"

Taking a sip of the wine, Nancy made a face and closed her eyes. "Medicinal purposes. My boss gave it to me for Christmas last year. I was going to give it away, but then put it away thinking that I just might need it someday."

Nodding her understanding, Melanie sipped her wine and leaned back on the sofa. Reflecting on the silence, she waited several minutes before telling Nancy the details of what had happened. They stayed up for another hour talking about the options that were open, hoping that Kyle Chandler would call and take the decision out of their hands. At eleven, Nancy declared that Kyle probably wasn't going to call, and even if he did, there was no reason they shouldn't go to sleep and deal with it if and when it happened.

Melanie agreed, and together they made up the sofa for her. Bidding each other good-night, Melanie took a quick shower and donned a silk nightshirt Nancy had given her and crawled into her makeshift bed.

She didn't think she'd be able to sleep with all the things on her mind, but exhaustion claimed her almost as soon as her head settled on the pillow.

Melanie awoke with a start. Shaking the cobwebs from her brain, she leaped from the sofa. What time was it? The clock in the kitchen told her it was six-forty-five. She groaned and then almost slapped her hand over her mouth. Was Mac awake? She tiptoed over to the bedroom door and peeked in. He was still asleep, the covers kicked off the bed, his big body sprawled across it diagonally.

Melanie folded the bedding she had used and replaced it in the linen closet. Needing to keep herself occupied, she went into the bathroom and brushed her teeth with her finger. She then brushed her auburn hair and twisted it into a French braid. After finishing with a light application of makeup from the cosmetics she carried in her purse, she quietly returned to the kitchen and began preparing breakfast. She had decisions to make. Not wanting to wake Nancy, she continued to prepare a morning meal for the three of them.

She was in the middle of chopping up fresh strawberries, bananas, grapes and melons for a fruit salad when it occurred to her that Mac might want something more substantial for breakfast. She glanced at the clock. Seven-thirty. He'd been asleep quite a long time. She walked to the bedroom door and gently pushed it open.

"Mac?"

He stirred and turned over, opening one eye and looking at her foggily. "Morning," he grunted, and flopped back over, burying his face in the pillow.

"Well," she said, leaning against the doorjamb. "Are you always this chipper in the mornings?"

The instant the words were out, she regretted them. How would he know?

"I don't know," Mac answered. "Don't you?"

Melanie prayed for divine intervention, but it wasn't to be. As she stood at the door looking embarrassed, Mac unwittingly came to her rescue. His eyes searched her pink face for an answer, but she couldn't force her voice to respond. Then he looked down at her hand.

"Hey, I hope you didn't take that the wrong way. I wouldn't want you to get mad or anything."

Melanie thought he had lost his fragile hold on his mind until she looked down and realized that she was still carrying the kitchen knife she had been using to slice the fruit. She pointed it at him, emphasizing her words.

"It would bode well for you to remember that, Wendell MacAuley Chandler. Now, what do you want for breakfast?"

He laughed and clasped his hands behind his head, causing the muscles of his chest—and in Melanie's stomach—to constrict.

"Surprise me."

She waved her knife and attempted calm. "I am having a fruit salad. If you want anything more, speak now or go hungry."

He laughed. "I guess I'd like some eggs if it's not too much trouble."

"It's not," she answered, and headed out the door, unaware that the light from the hallway made the shirt she was wearing practically invisible, until she heard a low whistle from Mac.

"None of that," she said, trying to give the appearance of normality. She doubted she would ever be normal again. If she ever had been. She indicated his duffel. "You can shower while I finish breakfast."

She slipped into Nancy's room and rummaged through her dresser drawer for clothes. Finding a pink T-shirt and a pair of jeans, she hurried getting dressed and didn't bother with shoes, pulling a pair of tennis socks on her feet.

A sleepy voice mumbled from beneath the covers. "Five more minutes."

Melanie laughed. "All right, but if you're late for school, don't blame me."

Nancy shot straight up. "I'm up."

"So's Mac. He's in the shower. Go back to sleep."

Grumbling, Nancy shook her head. "No, I'm awake now. Hey, those look familiar."

Looking at the clothes she had indicated, Melanie smiled. "Yes, well, I didn't think you'd mind. Of course, I had to roll up the legs on the jeans."

"Have you thought more about what we discussed last night?"

The serious tone in Nancy's voice stopped the smile on Melanie's face. "Yes, and I still don't think that being around here, cooped up all the time, will be good for Mac. If he's going to get his memory back quickly, he needs to be in a more relaxing atmosphere."

Nancy nodded. "All right. I don't think they'd ever be able to find him where you're going. But, are you sure that, uh, well, not to be a nay sayer, Mel, but you really don't know him."

Rolling her eyes, Melanie made a rude sound. "Please. It's not like I'm taking him on an illicit weekend to a tropic isle. I'm just getting him away from some men who are trying to kill him."

"Why should you do it?"

Stopping at the door, Melanie turned and looked at Nancy. Why was she doing it? She wasn't obligated to him. Or was she? "I have to, Nance. I can't let anyone take him away. I would worry. And I don't think anyone else could do any better than me. Except maybe his brother, and he isn't here."

With that, she left, and Nancy smiled at the closed door.

Melanie paused near the bathroom door when she heard the water running in the shower. *Melanie Rogers,* she told herself, *you are crazy. You don't even know that man and yet you've not only gotten yourself tangled up in a mess you don't understand, but you've dragged your best friend with you.* She knew she wanted to help protect Mac, but she didn't know why. Sure, he was great looking and sexy, and she was attracted to him ... or was it more than that? After meeting him only once? Was that really possible?

Melanie was setting the food on the table when Mac emerged from the bathroom. His dark hair was still damp from his shower, and it was curling around the edges. For some reason Melanie found that cute. He had replaced the small bandage near his left temple with a fresh one. He was wearing a pair of well-worn black jeans and a black-and-white striped polo shirt that had been in the duffel. Melanie told herself to put her eyes back into her head. He probably looked good in anything. And nothing.

"I guess I like scrambled eggs and toast." Mac smiled as he sat.

Melanie's head snapped up. Did he? She had no idea what he liked. Maybe he hated his eggs scrambled.

"Sorry about the light breakfast, Mac, but we're in a hurry."

He smiled and raised a glass of orange juice to his lips. Then a frown crossed his brow. "Mac? I thought you said my name was Wendell."

Melanie struggled to bury her laughter. "Well, actually it is Wendell, but—"

"But Mac is short for MacAuley?"

Melanie nodded. "And much more macho."

He grinned. "Am I a macho kind of guy?"

"I have no idea," she muttered. "Listen, Mac, I don't know whether it would be better to just tell you everything that's happened or let you remember it all on your own. I'm afraid that my limited knowledge might not do too much good anyway. I don't want to impede your recovery, but we have to work together from now on, so I have no choice."

He paused, then nodded. "So, what happened?"

A sigh of relief escaped her lips. "Well, I don't know the whole story myself, but I'll tell you what I know. You are a computer consultant. You live in Salem, and you are working in Bayview on a job. With WilCom." She watched his face for any signs of recognition.

He leaned back in his chair and touched the bandage near his temple. "How did this happen?"

"You were coming out of a telephone booth yesterday afternoon when you were grabbed by two men and driven to a scenic overlook near Lansport. Then one of them hit you over the head, and they had a gun—"

"Wait a minute," Mac interrupted. "You said some of this yesterday. But I thought I must have been wrong. This sounds too much like a crime show. Who were the men?"

"I don't know."

"Why did they kidnap me?"

"I don't know."

"Who prevented my untimely demise?"

Melanie twirled her fork in her fingers and tried to avoid his penetrating gaze.

"You did," he said, answering his own question.

"Well, I had to," she explained. "They could have killed you. I followed them in my car, and I made them think I had a gun. It was really a starter's pistol, but it has a bang, so how were they to know? And I made them put you in my car, and I took their car keys. I took you to the clinic in Lansport. Nancy hid the car while we were in the clinic. Then I went back to the square and got your car—"

She stopped when she saw the expression of disbelief on his face, and then waited for his reaction. He leaned over the table and took her hands, which were squeezed together, in his.

"Melanie, why didn't you call the police?"

Nancy appeared in the doorway. "We did. But they said that until you can remember what the men looked like, who they were or why they attacked you, there wasn't much they could do."

Mac nodded and rose, leaned on the counter and regarded the two women. Melanie glanced over at Nancy, who was now sitting at the table, picking through the fruit salad. After seeing her quick smile of encouragement, Melanie turned her gaze back to Mac and sighed.

"Nancy and I have done a lot of thinking, and we believe that you'd be safer away from Bayview and Lansport."

He frowned. "Because of those men?"

Nodding, Melanie took a step toward him. "Yes. We tried to contact your brother last night, but he wasn't home, so we left a message. Nancy will stay here and wait for his call. Then he can decide what should be done, or if you regain your memory, you can decide. And you can also explain to me just what has been going on around here."

Nancy rose and faced them. "I think that I will go and get some food for you for your trip. And maybe some clothes."

Melanie smiled gratefully. "Nancy, what would I do without you?"

They made up a list, and Nancy left, armed with credit cards, to shop for Melanie and Mac's trip.

His erupting laughter caught Melanie by surprise. "What?"

"Last night. That doctor called me Mr. Charles. Nick Charles. Does that make you Nora?"

Her eyes grew round. "How do you know that?"

"That is what I was wondering," he said, sobering. "Why is it that I can remember an old movie, but I can't remember my own name? And why did the doctor call me that?"

"Because that's what I told him," she stated as calmly as she could.

"I don't understand."

She sighed and sank down onto a chair. "I hope you won't be angry, but I, uh, let you believe certain things last night that weren't exactly true."

His eyes narrowed slightly as he looked at her. "About what?"

"About us."

"Us?" He definitely looked confused.

She drummed nervous fingers on the table. "Actually, Mac, I know that I let you believe we were sort of . . . well, together . . . but the truth is that we just met."

An expression very close to shock crossed his handsome features. "I don't believe it."

Melanie hadn't been sure what she expected, but this wasn't it. "It's true, Mac. I met you at WilCom yesterday. My sister, Liane, is a secretary there. You asked me out for a date, but then later that afternoon I saw you get kidnapped and . . ." Her voice trailed off at the look of bewilderment on his face.

"Then why did you do all this?" His arms flung out indicating his presence.

That was a good question. "I don't know, Mac. All I know is that when I saw those men shove you into that car, I just reacted. I jumped into my car and followed them. I was afraid that if I stopped to call the police, I would lose the car, and it's just as well that I didn't because of what could have happened at that overlook."

She looked down at her hands, waiting for his reaction. She heard something that sounded suspiciously like laughter. Jerking her head up, she saw him trying to contain his mirth.

"Just what is so funny, Wendell?"

He sat down and grasped her hands. "I'm sorry, but I just got this picture in my mind of me being protected by a fierce little guardian angel. I'm sorry I've been so much trouble, Melanie, and I haven't even thanked you."

She smiled. "You're welcome. But I really would appreciate it if your memory would return posthaste. I'm not used to being a guardian angel."

He lowered his head and kissed her lightly on the forehead. Then he was smiling at her. "I'm sorry our date was ruined. When I do get my memory back, I'll try to make it up to you. But for now, you really don't have to take me anywhere. If we aren't, well...involved, I don't think I should let you get into something so dangerous.''

Melanie felt disappointed. She had looked forward to being with Mac, even if he didn't remember anything. She couldn't give up so easily.

"I tell you what, Mac. You come with me, and if you get your memory back, we'll do whatever you say. And if you don't, and Nancy gets in touch with your brother, Kyle, then we'll do whatever he says. Okay?''

Mac considered her sincere expression for a moment, and then nodded. Melanie almost laughed aloud in relief. She didn't know why doing this for Mac was so important to her, but it was.

As he pitched in and helped her wash the dishes, they joked about things he could do to make up for all her troubles, but Melanie knew that she would never expect anything like that from him. And she knew she'd do it all again and more if he needed her.

Chapter Four

Believe me, Nance, if I thought there was a better option, I'd take it."

"Mmm...." Nancy was plotting. Melanie could hear it in her voice.

"I don't want you to do anything crazy while I'm gone, Nancy Doyle."

Soft laughter floated through the room. "Of course not, but that's only because you don't want to be left out."

Melanie rolled her eyes and studied the light fixture. "That's right. Besides, I need you to stick close to the phone. I need someone I trust to talk to Kyle Chandler."

"I'm so honored."

"You should be. It was either you or Liane."

"In that case, maybe I shouldn't be so honored."

As Mac walked into the room, Melanie was laughing. He stopped and smiled at her, and she nearly choked. Then he was picking up the suitcase Nancy had loaned Melanie and his own duffel. Melanie watched with unashamed pleasure as the muscles in his shoulders and arms rippled beneath the thin material of his polo shirt.

It was then Melanie realized that Nancy was singing, softly, and Melanie almost laughed out loud when she realized the song was "You Go to My Head."

"All right, you made your point," she said, silencing the concert.

"Maybe I should sing 'This is It'?" Nancy whispered.

"Maybe you should."

"Oh, this is great. I didn't want to pry, you know me, so quiet and unassuming—"

"So full of—"

"Now, now, none of that. What would Liane say?"

"Who do you think taught me all those words?"

They both laughed while Mac stood patiently waiting. Melanie gestured for him to put the bags down. "I have to make a phone call, Mac. I'll just be a minute."

As Mac leaned against the front doorjamb, Melanie picked up the phone. She had to call Liane.

After telling her that she wouldn't be able to help out with the swim meet, she said she would return the starter's pistol. Ignoring her older sister's protests, she continued.

"Liane, I need the keys to the cabin for a few days."

"Sort of a sudden vacation, isn't it?" her sister inquired. "I thought you were supposed to review a movie tomorrow."

Melanie groaned. She had forgotten all about it.

"I'll get it done. The movie opens in Bayview next Friday. The video of it is at the office. I have until Tuesday afternoon to get my copy in to Jim."

When her sister didn't say anything, Melanie knew that Liane was suspicious. Melanie never shrugged off her job responsibilities. Personally, she might be a mess of contradictions, but she never took her job lightly.

"I'm waiting," Liane said.

"What for?" Melanie asked.

"For you to tell me what is really wrong."

"Liane, I don't know half of it myself. Let me just say that Mac Chandler is in trouble and I'm helping him."

Liane's voice went up an octave. "What?" Then, before Melanie could answer, her sister was continuing. "How do you know? You weren't supposed to go out with him until tonight. What happened yesterday? Why would he need help from a total stranger?"

"I beg your pardon, Liane, but I am not a stranger, I'm your sister. I may act a little strange—"

"You know what I mean."

Mac walked over and indicated the bags and his watch, saying, "Are you still in a hurry?"

Melanie nodded, and Mac picked up the bags again and stood waiting. Liane's voice was now suspiciously low.

"Is he there now? Is Mac Chandler there? No one saw him around yesterday after lunch. What is going on? Melanie, this isn't like you! Have you done something you're going to regret?"

Melanie laughed at her sister's protectiveness and said ruefully, "Probably, Liane, but there's not much I can do about it now. I want you to listen carefully. Meet me at the junction of the highway to the cabin. Bring the keys with you. Bye."

She hung up the telephone before her sister could ask any more questions.

"Is your sister overprotective?" Mac inquired.

Melanie and Nancy laughed. "You could say that," Nancy answered. "Liane is a victim of the mother-hen syndrome. Melanie and her two brothers are her little chicks."

Melanie picked up her purse and smiled. "You'd think that mothering her own kids would be enough, but not for Liane."

They said goodbye to Nancy and walked to her car in the driveway. It had been decided that since both Mac's and Melanie's cars had been seen it would be better to take Nancy's. Mac insisted on driving, and Melanie couldn't talk him out of it.

Melanie sighed her acquiescence and gave him the directions to the junction.

She turned the radio on, and they talked about music, which, for some strange reason, Mac could remember. As they neared the scenic overlook where Mac had almost died, Melanie felt her body tense, and she glanced over at Mac to discover that he, too, looked tense and wary.

"Something happened around here," he said as he slowed down.

Melanie swallowed hard and nodded. "I don't think we should stop, but this is where you lost your memory."

He stared out the windshield at the overlook and ran his fingers through his hair in a gesture of frustration. Melanie could see him straining for the memories that wouldn't come to him. She reached over and squeezed his hand reassuringly.

"Hey, don't worry about it. The doctor said that your memory will return in time. Trying too hard might do more harm than good."

He turned and looked into her eyes, then he nodded and tried to smile.

"Yeah, you're right, but it's so hard not to try."

Melanie nodded. "I know, but just try not to think about it. Think about something else."

"Like what?" he said softly, so that Melanie knew exactly what he was thinking. She had to struggle to keep from throwing herself across the small distance that separated them and into his arms.

"Think about anything that won't cause you to wreck Nancy's car."

He chuckled and put his eyes back on the road as he accelerated the car past the overlook. It was only another ten minutes until they approached the junction.

They had barely pulled off the road behind her sister's station wagon before Liane was out the door and stalking over to confront them.

"Melanie Eileen Rogers! How dare you hang up before I was finished—"

"Liane, not now," Melanie said, forcing a smile as Mac rounded the front of Nancy's Mazda. Liane glanced over at him suspiciously.

"Hello, Mac."

Melanie groaned inwardly. "You will have to excuse my sister, Mac. But she is of a suspicious nature."

"Really?" he said lightly, stepping back from Liane, who had the grace to blush and look embarrassed.

"I am not," she claimed with all the calm she could muster. "But you have yet to explain to me what is going on. And why are you driving Nancy's car?"

Melanie glanced briefly at Mac before saying, "Liane, Mac had—an accident yesterday. He can't remember anything."

Liane's amber eyes grew round with wonder as she turned to look at Mac.

"Really?" Liane said, her gaze zeroing in on the bandage above Mac's left temple. "What happened?"

Melanie looked over her shoulder, expecting to see a dark car. She did not want to waste time standing around telling Liane what had happened. It would only cause her to worry.

"Liane, I will explain it all to you later, but right now, I need the keys to the cabin." She pulled the starter's pistol out of her purse and handed it to her temporarily placated sister. She thought about the real gun laying at the bottom of her suitcase and wondered crazily what she would have done if she'd mixed them up.

"All right, but I just want to say right now that I do not approve—"

"Liane, you rarely do. You're a stick-in-the-mud."

Melanie almost laughed out loud as her older sister pulled herself up in a stance of mock righteous indignation. She pulled a key ring with several keys on it from her jeans pocket.

"Here," she said evenly. Then in a low voice, "I want details when next we speak, sister."

Melanie hugged Liane swiftly and whispered to her, "I will give you all the details I can. I promise."

Turning back to Mac, who was leaning against the front fender of the car, she smiled. "All set."

He waved at Liane. "Nice seeing you."

Liane smiled tentatively. "I hope you're better soon."

"So do I," he said, and climbed into the car next to Melanie. As they pulled back onto the road, Melanie directed him to head east.

"Where are we going?" Mac asked as soon as they were on the highway.

"We are going east from here to the mountains and a cabin Liane and I own. It used to belong to our parents. They bought it just a few months before they died. I haven't been there very often."

Mac looked over at her and then put his hand over hers and gave it a light squeeze.

"Have you lived here all your life?" he asked cheerfully.

"Yes and no," she answered. "I was born in Seattle. My parents moved here when I was about ten. I went to college at the University of Oregon. I traveled during my vacations. San Diego, Los Angeles, Reno, Denver, New Orleans, Dallas, Phoenix, Sacramento, San Francisco. Then, after I graduated, I returned to Bayview."

Mac seemed impressed. "You've done a lot for someone so young."

Melanie smiled back at him. "I'll bet you've done more."

"Ah," he said. "But I'm older than you."

His laughter joined hers, and she felt herself relax a little.

They spent most of the daylight hours driving. It was approximately three hundred miles across the Oregon wilderness and mountains to the beautiful area where Melanie's parents had purchased their retirement cabin. It was almost six in the evening when Melanie and Mac pulled in front of the rustic cabin nestled into the mountainside.

"Hey, this is great," Mac enthused as he carried the luggage up the wide porch steps. Melanie unlocked the front door with one hand, holding a bag of groceries in her other arm.

"I'm sorry," Melanie said as she walked through the cabin into the kitchen and set the bag of groceries on the counter. "But there's no electricity. Liane and her family use this place as a base camp, cooking over the fireplace and camp stoves. There's a small gas generator that provides power for a small fridge and the running water, but we'll have to use lanterns and candles for light."

Mac set the suitcase and his duffel inside the door and shut it.

"Don't be sorry," he said, looking over the large room. "There's more atmosphere this way."

"More romantic," Melanie muttered as she unloaded the groceries.

"What did you say?" He was right behind her!

"I said we had better fix dinner before our perishables perish."

"Sure you did," he said, and went back into the main room. Melanie left the food sitting on the counter and followed him. She stopped at the kitchen door and watched him. He was looking at the room. Her gaze followed his to the rough-cut walls, built-in bookcases, sturdy furniture, wood floor, stone fireplace. At the rear of the cabin were two doors. A bedroom and a bathroom. Mac turned and saw Melanie watching him. She knew at that moment exactly what he was thinking. One bedroom.

"My parents had planned on converting the attic area into a loft and wiring the place for electricity, but they never got around to it."

She wondered crazily why she felt she had to explain anything to Mac. She had lots of platonic relationships with men and wouldn't have felt in the least uncomfortable with any of them in a similar situation. But this was different. She'd never had to contend with someone like Mac. With those other men she'd just felt like one of the guys. With Mac, she felt like a woman.

She had noticed other men before, but none had ever made her feel this sense of oneness, this excitement she felt whenever she looked into his deep black eyes. She felt herself drawn to this man she didn't know, but did know, and who didn't know her. She was afraid of getting too attached to someone she knew so little about, but she couldn't stop herself, and she wasn't sure she even should try. She wondered if it weren't already too late for that.

She suddenly realized that she had just been standing in the doorway, staring at Mac. A blush crept up her neck, and she stepped back.

"Why don't you put the bags near the fireplace while I start the generator, and then we'll fix dinner?"

He nodded thoughtfully and walked toward the bags. Melanie slipped outside to the small shed attached to the house to start the generator. When she returned, Mac was setting out the food for their meal. Salad fixings, French bread, three kinds of cheese and a bottle of red wine.

"Well, what do you want me to do?" he asked. "I am not known for my culinary skills."

"What skills are you known for?" she teased. Then she suddenly realized that Mac had remembered something. It was small, and probably insignificant, but it was a step in the right direction. She looked at his happy face as he began slicing the tomatoes, and she knew that he hadn't noticed his progress. Not wanting to talk about the subject of his amnesia, Melanie directed her attention to the meal and made small talk about how her parents had found the cabin and how she and Liane took turns using it.

While Melanie gathered the dishes and utensils, Mac brought in some wood and started a fire in the stone fireplace, which took up most of one wall in the living room. He positioned the couch and coffee table in front of the fireplace and put two candlesticks on the table. Melanie showed him where the candles were kept, and while he lit the candles, she carried out the food.

The sun was setting, and shadows were lengthening outside. The glow from the fire and the candles made the room blaze with warmth and intimacy. Melanie felt herself being drawn into the romantic setting as Mac poured the wine and held his glass up to touch hers. As she sipped the warm wine, she smiled at him and wondered if their date would have been like this.

They talked for a long while about anything Mac could remember. Melanie felt that she was actually getting to know him. Then she remembered that the Mac she was getting to know might not be the same Mac when his full memory returned.

Mac was gazing at the fire as they sat close to each other on the couch.

"I know the doctor said that it was just a matter of time, but what if I never get all of my memory back? What if I stay just like this?"

Melanie reached across the small gap separating them and touched his shoulder.

"That won't happen. You'll be fine. But if it does, you'll go on. You'll relearn the parts you can, and then make new memories."

Mac sighed and took her hand in his, squeezing it gently. "Then I guess I'll just have to start making those new memories. I don't suppose you'd be willing to lend me any of yours?"

Melanie grinned and wrinkled her nose. "I suppose I could spare a few. Returnable, of course, when your own return."

She just hoped it wouldn't all end with the return of his memory. The longer she knew MacAuley Chandler, the more she wanted to know him. They sat on the couch staring into the fire for a long while, neither wanting to break the spell of the moment. Finally, they knew they had to, and moved to clear away their dishes.

After they had washed the dishes and returned to the living room, she retrieved her purse and joined him on the couch.

"I thought that maybe some of the things you had with you might help your memory."

Mac nodded slowly and watched as she withdrew the items from her purse. She took out his wallet and opened it.

"Do you know what date you were born?"

Mac rested his elbow on the back of the couch and touched his fingers to his right temple. He shook his head. Melanie debated between telling him and letting him remember on his own.

"How about where you live?"

He seemed to be chasing a thought that refused to be captured. "You know," he said slowly, "it's almost as if everything is right in front of me and just out of reach. Like it isn't in focus. You said that I lived in Salem before coming to WilCom?"

Melanie nodded. Mac frowned.

"I don't know. Jefferson? Washington? I feel like I'm reciting a history lesson. Monroe? Why does that seem so familiar?"

Melanie touched his knee. "You lived on Monroe Street in Salem. Mac, you're beginning to remember. Do you want to go on?"

He nodded and she began going through his wallet, pulling out various cards and the pictures.

He stared at the pictures of his family for a long time, turned them over and read the inscriptions. He fought for recognition, but it wouldn't come.

Melanie took the items and returned them to his wallet. "You're trying too hard. Don't think that it will all come back in a few minutes."

Mac sighed and agreed. "I guess you're right. It's frustrating not to know, but at the same time, with the truth is bound to come things I would rather not remember at all."

He touched his head gingerly, and Melanie could tell that another headache was causing him some pain.

"I think you should take another one of those pills the doctor gave you." She reached into her purse and handed him the bottle.

Mac's brows drew together. "Why?"

"Because your head hurts, that's why." At his quizzically amused gaze, Melanie closed her eyes and spoke dramatically. "I am a psychic. There is nothing you can hide from the Great Melanac."

She felt his hands on her shoulders, and her eyes flew open in surprise. His smile was different, sort of lazy. One dark eyebrow rose as her eyes widened. "I guess you're not as all-knowing as you thought," he murmured, just before his lips touched hers.

He pulled away just as Melanie began to melt against him and headed into the kitchen with his pills. She heard water running and, by the time he returned the pills to her for safekeeping, she thought she'd stopped shaking. He paused after she had taken the bottle and looked at her.

"You know, I don't remember getting undressed last night. Yet I woke up practically naked. Do you think my memory losses are pervading into present time?"

Melanie cocked an eyebrow and tried to look admonishing. "I think that your memory loss hasn't dulled your sense of mischief. Now, go on. I'll sleep on the couch."

He looked as if he was about to argue with her until she pointed firmly at the bedroom door.

Grinning, he saluted sharply and turned a little too quickly, staggering a step or two. She didn't say a word after she saw him stop and then start again, very slowly.

She put out the fire, taking her time, and then went to all the windows, securing the locks and then the front door, even though she knew that there was no real reason to do so up here. Still, she wouldn't feel safe under the circumstances if she didn't take these precautions.

Then she went into the bathroom to prepare for bed. After washing her face and brushing her teeth, she made up the couch with linens that were stored in a cedar chest window box. She slid beneath the covers and stared into the dark room. She hoped she was doing the right thing.

Melanie regained consciousness slowly. Something was wrong. No, not wrong. Different. The first of her senses to awake was her sense of smell. She was smelling food!

Melanie tentatively opened her eyes and found Mac watching her. He was leaning over the back of the couch, his fingers wound through a lock of her hair. He seemed to be contemplating it quite intensely.

"You know," he said softly, twirling the strands of hair in a ray of sunshine, "your hair changes color magnificently in the sun. It's almost as if the fire of the sun is alive in each strand." He looked down into her eyes, and Melanie knew she would have collapsed if she hadn't already been lying down.

She swallowed with some difficulty when she realized he wasn't making any move to release her. He frowned and dropped her hair as his hand went to the small bandage on his head.

"How do you feel?" Melanie whispered. She suddenly wondered if he had regained his memory overnight.

"Well, I guess I'm fine," he said thoughtfully.

"And you haven't remembered anything else?" She held her breath, waiting for his answer. It didn't come right away, as his gaze seemed to be roaming over her body.

"I may not remember much, but I've obviously got good taste in women."

Melanie blushed and smiled.

His forefinger then traced the line of her jaw, working its way toward her lips. She was totally mesmerized by his black eyes and his long, tanned fingers. Her breathing became shallow, then stopped altogether. Mac lowered his lips to hers.

It was a gentle, exploratory kiss. Melanie's mind went on hold temporarily as she gave herself up to the kiss, sighing and opening her lips under his. His tongue slid into her mouth and touched her teeth, the roof of her mouth, the sensitive spot under her tongue. Melanie moaned, and slid her arms up to his neck, enjoying the feel of his short silky hair under her fingertips.

She couldn't believe the sensations he brought to life in her. Her skin actually tingled, and she could have sworn her lips were burning.

Mac suddenly jerked back and ran into the kitchen. A cloud of smoke was emanating from the hot-plate. Well, at least something was burning. Melanie laughed to herself as she got her things and went into the bathroom.

When she emerged from the shower ten minutes later, dressed in jeans and a sweatshirt, with light makeup on her fresh face, Mac was sitting at the kitchen table, drinking instant coffee. The unburned portion of breakfast was on the table. Melanie didn't mention the still-smoky kitchen and sat down to eat.

A slow drizzle was turning into a light shower, and Melanie gazed out at the gray sky. It looked like the beginning of a long rainstorm. What were they going to do all day? Sit around and stare at each other?

A few minutes later Mac rose and rinsed his coffee cup. Then he turned to her, rubbing his hands together.

"So," he announced. "Got a deck of cards?"

Melanie laughed aloud. She could have kissed him for being so understanding. Considering that a good idea, she reached up and surprised Mac by kissing him loudly on the cheek.

They spent the day inside playing games. Poker, with peanuts for money, gin, hearts, go fish. When they had tired of card games, they moved on to board games. Liane had brought several for her children on their last visit. There was Monopoly, in which Melanie wound up as a land baron with Mac as a migrant worker; there was a rousing game of Sorry, which they almost never finished for knocking each other's men off the board; and Trivial Pursuit, which they played as a way to help Mac's recall.

It worked, to a degree. By the third round he had remembered his third-grade teacher's name and the name of his dog when he was young. But then, he couldn't decide which was Mrs. Jarrold and which was Ginger.

In the late afternoon, after a lunch of peanut-butter sandwiches and fruit punch, they played I spy and twenty questions. When the rain stopped, they cheered and ran outside, only to sink into the mud next to the porch. They came back into the rapidly darkening cabin and lit some kerosene lanterns and candles, and suddenly, the atmosphere shifted from fun and games to a quiet, romantic tension.

Melanie then sought diversions, such as scrounging up something for dinner to keep her mind off Mac. It didn't work very well, but it kept her hands busy and her mouth shut.

When she had finished preparing their meager meal, she carried it on a tray into the living room and found Mac, on one knee, coaxing a fire to life. Melanie sighed inwardly. He certainly wasn't making this any easier.

She set the tray on the coffee table and knelt beside it. Mac walked over and knelt opposite her. They ate in relative silence. Melanie was so full of thoughts and emotions from her day with Mac that she wasn't sure what she should do. She felt that she had learned a lot about him during the day, about the way he thought and felt about so many different subjects. But, at the same time, she didn't feel that she had learned anything because, without his complete recall, how could she really know anything about him?

As she gazed into the fire, she felt Mac's eyes on her. She turned slowly to face him and found his eyes boring into her own. What was he thinking? Could he read her thoughts? She hoped not, because she was thinking that she was falling in love with this stranger who didn't seem like a stranger.

Chapter Five

Mac looked into her large hazel eyes, shining in the firelight, as he searched her face. Melanie stared at him, hoping he would get his memory back and, in the same thought, hoping he wouldn't for a while. She felt as though she knew this Mac and that he understood her. She was wary of starting over again with the other Mac. The Mac who had asked her out for dinner. Was he like this Mac? The Mac she was with now, the one with the intense look in his dark eyes and the open way he had accepted his situation and her, might be nothing like the Mac she had met at WilCom. She could trust this Mac. What if, when his memory returned, Mac turned out to be a chauvinistic womanizer without a shred of sincerity or compassion? Her mind balked. No. Amnesia couldn't restructure a personality. Could it?

"What are you thinking?" Mac's voice broke through her thoughts, and its deep sensual sound chased away her doubts. "Your eyes reflect every emotion you feel. You know that, don't you?" Melanie shook her head. This would never do. Because what she was thinking right now had nothing to do with Mac's mental state. Rather, it focused upon his physical state. And he was in a fine physical state. Her gaze kept drifting to the strong tanned column of his neck and the small patch of chest she could see where his polo shirt was unbuttoned.

"The fire's going out," she said weakly, in an attempt to divert him.

The heavy lidded gaze of his dark eyes almost made Melanie melt right into the couch.

"Oh, I think that the fire is just getting started."

She was afraid to speak, afraid to move. She knew that whatever she did would reveal what she felt. She was falling in love with him. And she couldn't stop it. She didn't want to. Melanie had been falling in love with the idea of being in love for so long that now it was extremely easy to let Mac draw her the rest of the way. Her doubts weren't about her own feelings, but whether Mac could return those feelings.

Mac was looking at her with the quizzical stare again. "Why is it," he began, carefully choosing his words, "that I feel so incredibly comfortable with you? Why do I feel as though I could tell you anything? And that you would understand?"

Melanie blinked rapidly at the tears forming in her eyes. He didn't know it, but he was describing exactly how she felt.

Then he stood and put another log on the fire. Melanie tried to use the time to gather control of the rapidly deteriorating restraint that had seen her through twenty-two years of temptation. She almost laughed out loud. That she had never been tempted was becoming patently clear. It had been so easy to avoid serious relationships for so long simply because she had never met any man who turned her bones to butter. What she was feeling for Mac was totally foreign to her. But she knew instinctively that it was what she had been waiting for all these years. She had been waiting for him.

As Melanie watched the muscles of Mac's back move as he arranged the logs with the poker, she wondered if maybe it wasn't just a physical thing. But, even to her inexperienced ears, that sounded stupid.

He turned and walked back to where she sat, settling himself beside her. She didn't resist when he pulled her into his arms, and when his lips touched hers, she was lost to the sensations only he could create.

She felt his hands sliding down her back and her leg, then returning, and she wondered vaguely how she could feel his hand on her bare skin through her clothes.

Suddenly, he pulled away and looked at her. His expression was confused. Then he rose and began to pace. Melanie sat on the couch and stared dazedly at him.

"What's wrong?" she asked when she finally found her voice.

He stopped pacing and faced her. His face was brooding. "I am suddenly wondering what kind of woman would take a total stranger away with her to such a secluded place. If what you've told me is true, I can't believe that you wouldn't think about what could happen to you."

Wide hazel eyes stared at him. Tears threatened, but she blinked them away. She shook her head.

"I told you why we had to leave."

"No," he said. "You told me why I had to leave. Something about my having something these guys wanted and that they'd stop at nothing to get it."

"That's right."

"That's why I had to get away. But not why you had to stay with me. From what you've told me, you don't even know me. Are you so naive that you trust strangers all the time, or do you make a habit of inviting strange men to go away with you for weekends?"

Melanie stared in astonishment. Of all the nerve! Her hurt at being pushed away was rapidly supplanted by anger, and she fought to keep her voice calm.

"Are you upset because I cared enough to help you?"

"No, of course not," he snapped. "I just wonder why you brought me with you here?"

She pulled her feet beneath her and returned his glare. "Because you were in trouble and needed to get away. Those people want something from you, and until you remember what it is, you're safer if you're away. And no one could know you're here."

Mac was shaking his head. "If you were concerned for my safety, why didn't you just tell the police to protect me? Or for that matter, why didn't you just leave me at a hospital?"

Her hazel eyes narrowed as she considered his words. "I didn't leave you with the police because they aren't equipped to handle something like this in Bayview. It isn't that they don't do a good job of keeping the general peace of the county, but let's be realistic. There isn't much major crime being perpetrated in Bayview. The same goes for the hospital. It would have been too easy for those men to get to you in a hospital." She paused, confusion creasing her smooth brow. "Why are you acting like this? I thought you understood—"

"I understand the necessity, Melanie. What I don't understand is why you took it upon yourself to do it."

"Because I was there," she retorted. "I saw what happened, I heard what those men said. They could be after me, now, too. And since you were hardly in any condition to make decisions, I made them. Maybe I'm vain, but I think I've done a pretty good job of protecting you so far."

His bark of laughter jarred her nerves. "I'm not disputing that, Melanie. What I want to know is who you thought was going to protect you?"

She stared blankly at him. "Protect me from what? I told you they can't know we're here."

"Who could you count on to protect yourself against me?"

He'd said them softly, but his words were as hard as diamonds. She gazed up into his hardened features and decided that if he had been trying to frighten her, he had failed.

"I don't need protection from you, Mac," she stated calmly.

"How do you know that?" he ground out.

She shrugged. "Because I trust you. I know you wouldn't hurt me."

He began pacing, stopping every few feet to swear or yell at her. "How could you trust someone you just met?"

"I could say that I have a sixth sense about people, but I won't. I am a good judge of character, though."

"So," he said sarcastically, "every time you meet a guy who passes your character test, you invite him to spend the weekend with you?"

"Of course, I don't," Melanie interrupted, her voice rising. "You don't understand. I've never—that is, I don't—" Her confusion was making her angry. "You wouldn't hurt me!" she repeated.

Mac was looking at her as though she were crazy. Which, of course, was exactly how she felt—how he made her feel. His frustrated sigh forced her eyes back to his.

"But how could you know that?" he asked. "I don't even know that. And even if I wasn't going to murder you, didn't you think it was a gamble coming to a place like this with a man you don't know? Haven't you learned anything about men? What kind of relationships have you had that left you so naive?"

When she stared helplessly at him, his eyes widened in disbelief. "Melanie," he said, his voice suddenly quiet.

"Have you never . . . ?" He left the question hanging. Melanie felt gauche and ignorant.

"No, Mac, I have never had sex with anyone. Don't feel you have to tiptoe around the subject. I may not have actually done it, but I do know what it is."

"How old are you?" He sounded incredulous.

Melanie jumped to her feet. "What has that got to do with anything?"

"Just curious," he said, sinking back on the couch. "Do you mind if I ask why?"

Melanie stared down at him. "Why?"

"Yes, why? I mean, are you saving yourself for marriage or what?"

"Or what," she answered, her hands on her hips.

"What does that mean?" he asked quietly.

"It means that I have never met a man I cared enough about to share my—" She stopped when she saw the laughter shaking his body. Indignation flared in her body. "How dare you laugh at me, *Wendell* Chandler!"

He rose swiftly and grabbed her upper arms before she could turn away. "I wasn't laughing at you exactly, Melanie. It was just those intellectual words you were using to describe passion. And you are passionate, Melanie. I know that from the way you react when I hold you in my arms. Don't intellectualize what you're feeling. Just feel. And don't ever be afraid of your emotions or of expressing them."

"I don't see what that has to do with—"

"Melanie, why don't you just say what you mean?"

She was almost afraid to ask. "And what would that be?"

He was smiling that smile again, and Melanie felt her knees melting. "That would be that I am the only man who has ever really turned you on. And that was the reason you brought me up here. Why you 'trusted' me. If you hadn't been attracted to me, we'd still be back in Bayview."

Melanie's face was burning at his rather crude, albeit accurate account of the way she felt. She opened her mouth to try to deny his words, but her lips were suddenly closed by two of his fingers.

"Don't try to deny it, Melanie, you just blushed three shades of red that I could see just by firelight."

He then replaced his fingers with his lips, and Melanie knew that if he hadn't been holding her, she would have crumpled onto the floor into a heap at his feet. She opened her mouth willingly when she felt his tongue sliding along her lips. Her hands crept up between them along his chest and paused to run through the chest hair that was nestled in the V of his shirt before coming to rest on either side of his neck. Her fingers were sensitive to every muscle and every inch of skin they touched.

While his lips continued their gentle assault on hers, his hands left her arms and began moving on her back. She hadn't worn a bra under her sweatshirt, and Mac's growling sigh of satisfaction when his roaming hands discovered this fact sent a thrill of desire coursing through Melanie's body. She tightened her hold on his neck and arched her body into his. His hands had worked their way underneath her shirt and were caressing her bare skin, sending electric currents along her spine. She felt his lips leave hers, but before she could do more than gasp for air, he was kissing a trail from her lips to her ear. She suddenly realized that she was pulling his shirt out of the waistband of his jeans, her hands boldly running over his waist to his back. She felt him draw a shuddering breath and drag his lips away from her throat.

"Look, Melanie, I think we should stop."

She stared at him, struggling for composure. "You don't want me?" Her words sounded far away.

"Do you even have to ask?"

She didn't; she felt the evidence of his arousal. She shook her head, but the confusion was still in her wide eyes.

"Melanie," he said, "I'm not sure you really know what you're doing—"

She jerked away with all the dignity she could muster. "How dare you patronize me, MacAuley Chandler! I am over twenty-one. Old enough to decide for myself whether or not I want to make love with someone!" She stepped away from him and drew herself up to her full height.

"Maybe it is you who isn't really sure of what you are doing," she challenged. "After all, if you can't remember who you are, you can't remember sex, either!"

She stormed off toward the bathroom, but his voice echoed behind her. "Maybe I just didn't want you and your ideals to get hurt."

She whirled around, peering at him through the shadowy darkness. "What is that supposed to mean?"

"Just that I may not be the man you need, Melanie. If you've waited this long before giving yourself to a man, you obviously had reasons, and one of them was probably that you wanted to be in love."

He had intended to help her see things more objectively, but his words only incensed her more. She stormed back over to where he stood.

"How dare you presume to know how I feel. About you or anything else. You don't even know me! And if I want to fall in love with you, I damn well will, and there's not a blessed thing you can do about it!"

Leaving him astonished and speechless, she whirled back around and stomped back to the bathroom, grabbing a candle on her way.

She slammed the door behind her and set the candle on the vanity. She had washed her face, brushed her teeth and gotten undressed before she realized what she had said. She was buttoning the shirt she had slept in the night before and muttering to herself about presumptuous men when she stopped and stared at herself in the mirror. Shadows danced eerily around her reflection. She picked up her hairbrush and looked down at it. Her hand was trembling. *Oh, no,* she thought. *I practically told him I was in love with him.*

She muttered an unladylike expletive and began to vigorously brush her hair.

When he knocked on the door, she screamed, and the hairbrush went flying into the bathtub. Its clatter seemed to echo forever.

"Are you all right?" he asked from the other side of the closed door.

Melanie took a deep breath and tried to calm her nerves. "I am just fine. I just don't like people sneaking up on me and pounding on doors." She looked around the bathroom vainly for a robe, but knew before she looked that she had not packed one. Well, it wasn't as if he hadn't already seen her like this, she told herself as she reached over and retrieved the hairbrush. She dropped it back into her overnight case and then picked up her dirty clothes and put them into the laundry bag she had packed. She then turned and jerked the door open, walking out with her back ramrod straight past Mac, who was leaning on the wall outside the door.

"Nice outfit," he murmured.

"Thank you," she said, her bare feet gliding along the polished wood toward the bedroom door. Just the sound of his voice set the pit of her stomach to clenching. When she reached the door, she realized that she had left her candle in the bathroom. She decided that she would rather stumble in the dark than walk past Mac again. "You get the couch tonight," she said over her shoulder, closing the bedroom door with a click behind her.

She made her way over to the bed and discovered that Mac had turned it down. *He is so sweet,* she thought, then checked herself. *No, he is not. He is a jerk. And if he doesn't want me, he just doesn't know what he's missing.* She heard the water running in the bathroom. "I hope you cut yourself shaving," she muttered. As she got into bed, she continued to talk to herself. "Big dope thinks I'm naive just because I haven't had sex." She punched her pillow several times and tried to get comfortable. "At least I waited until I—" She broke off as she realized what she had been about to say. *Until I fell in love with someone.*

I am not in love, she told herself firmly. *I'm just in lust. I'd react this way to any good-looking man with a body like that, right?* "Wrong," she said out loud. She had met plenty of men who fit that description, but none had ever caused this turmoil in her emotions. Maybe it was just as well Mac had backed off, she tried to convince herself. Who needed his psychoanalysis anyway?

She was still muttering to herself about men and their bossy natures and their stubborn egos and their know-it-all attitudes when she heard the bathroom door open and close. She almost fell out of bed when he knocked on the bedroom door.

She tried to sound casual, but her voice was distinctly breathy when she asked, "What do you want?"

"I didn't mean to insult you, Melanie." His voice was low, and Melanie felt her anger ebbing. She had never been able to stay angry at anyone for very long, and she was finding it even harder to stay angry at Mac, especially when he soothed her prickly emotions with his sexy voice.

"I know you didn't, Mac," she said, keeping her voice even and as unemotional as possible. "But I really do know how to look after myself."

"You know, Melanie, I might be a total jerk when I get my memory back."

"Trying to give yourself an out?"

"No. I just wanted to make sure you know what I'm thinking. The future is very unsure for me. You may not want to be a part of it."

Melanie sighed. "You big dope. You're a computer consultant, not a syndicate crime boss."

She could feel his smile, even though she couldn't see it through the door. "Melanie?"

"Hmm?"

"Are you really falling in love with me?"

She was glad he couldn't see her face. She sighed. "Go to sleep, Mac."

His soft laughter warmed her, and she smiled as she snuggled down into the covers. She drifted off to sleep with only good thoughts of Mac flitting through her mind. She really was falling in love, she thought contentedly as sleep claimed her.

Chapter Six

The sound was suspiciously like a wooden spoon banging on the bottom of a frying pan. Then came a chorus of "Rise and Shine/and give God your glory."

The bedroom door was flung open, and Mac marched around the room, banging on a pan and singing at the top of his lungs. Melanie stared for a moment, then buried her head beneath her pillow, laughing.

"Come on, you lazeabout," he boomed. "It's a beautiful day, and I think I'm suffering from cabin fever."

Melanie peeked out from under the pillow. "And what is it that you would like to do today, Mr. Chandler?"

He leaned over her and grinned, waggling his eyebrows.

Melanie laughed. "Besides that."

"Oh, you mean I have to pick something else?"

She pushed him away, laughing, happy that he wasn't bringing up the previous night.

"Get up and shower your luscious body, wench. There are unexplored venues to explore."

With that, he was gone, and Melanie got up, shaking her head at his antics. She had been worried that he would be moody and somber, but her own mood had lightened considerably when he had played the fool for her instead. She knew that it was probably just to make her more comfortable with him, and she felt her heart open to him even more.

After a light breakfast of orange juice and fire-toasted English muffins with cream cheese, they decided to hike into the mountains and have a picnic. They packed fruit and cheese and crackers and soda, along with a thermos of soup, into two small backpacks left by Liane's children. Adding a loaf of bread and jam to the packs, they set off into the woods.

Following a day of confinement in the cabin, the sunshine seemed brighter and more beautiful than ever. Melanie had taken her camera and several rolls of film, and stopped frequently to snap pictures, determined to return with as many photographs as she could manage. Mac's words played through her mind, though she tried to block them. What if she really didn't want to be a part of his life after he got his memory back? Her heart balked at the idea, for she could see no instance that could make her shy away.

Mac's feelings, however, were what made Melanie wonder. What if he didn't want her in his life when his memory returned? What if he were married or engaged? What if his life in Salem offered him more than what she could offer? She wasn't very sophisticated, and she wasn't a nightlife person. She was more a home-and-hearth kind of person.

She grimaced to herself. That was always what she accused Liane of being. Now she thought that maybe she owed her sister an apology for the flippant remarks she had made. Liane was in love and happy; she had a lot more than most people. And Melanie didn't want to be one of those people. She wanted to be in love and to have a family. And she wanted Mac to be a part of her life. She gave up one quiet, heartfelt sigh, then made a conscious effort to enjoy the day she *did* have with Mac. She allowed the scenery to distract her from her doubts, and she smiled in wonder at what was around her.

The majestic mountains of the Malheur National Forest caused Melanie and Mac to speak in hushed tones. It seemed almost sacrilegious to speak above a whisper when walking through such a magnificent example of nature's beauty. In mutual harmony, they walked by several beautiful areas, undecided as to where to have their picnic.

After hiking for three hours, Mac feigned exhaustion and opted for the next open area he saw. He dropped to his knees with his backpack beside him. "This is a wonderful spot for a picnic, wouldn't you say?"

Melanie looked around at the small clearing, which had no view of the mountains, and remembered that a stream was another half mile up the trail. "On your feet, soldier," she ordered. "We have another half mile before we can stop. Believe me, it'll be worth it."

She started to turn away, but stopped when she saw the faraway look in Mac's eyes. It was a strange expression, one Melanie hadn't seen before. She knew, even as she looked at him, that it was the real Mac. The inner struggle of thoughts was there in his beautiful dark eyes. She knew that his memory had to return sometime, but she wanted, needed, more time.

She put her backpack on a rock and stood perfectly still, watching the emotions play across his handsome features. After a couple of minutes, he dropped his penetrating gaze to the ground and poked at the root of a tree with a stick. Melanie realized that she was holding her breath, and let it out slowly. Mac suddenly looked up and smiled.

"Well," he said, "let's go then." With that, he rose swiftly and gracefully to his feet and set out on the trail, leaving Melanie standing with her mouth open.

As she stared at his broad back, she felt guilty at being glad that he hadn't gotten his memory back. She was grateful for the extra time she had been given, but she also knew that anything less than a lifetime would be too short.

Ten minutes later, they were standing beside a rushing stream, overlooking a large meadow, the mountains in the background. It was worth the extra time. Melanie smiled to herself as she removed her backpack and retrieved her camera. She snapped several pictures of the landscape and a few of Mac before he realized what she was up to. Then she laughed and breathed in a lungful of the fresh mountain air. Her gaze returned to Mac, and she found him looking at her, a curious expression in his eyes.

"What?" she asked.

He smiled. "This is better," he explained. "You were right."

Melanie wasn't at all sure that was what he meant, but she returned his smile, and they settled in for their picnic. "Remember that next time."

Her words had been offhand, but it wasn't until after she had uttered them that she recognized the implication. She assumed they would be returning together someday. And with sudden clarity she knew she could never return without Mac. This place and the cabin would always hold a special place in her heart, and it would always be associated with what she was sharing with Mac this weekend. He didn't seem to notice.

"Have to get the electricity hooked up," he added as Melanie pulled herself away from negative thoughts. She laughed and shook her head.

"No, I don't think so. I like it the way it is."

"Do you?" His voice was soft, like a caress, and Melanie shivered.

"Cold?" he asked. She shook her head and smiled, sitting down on the red-checked picnic tablecloth they had brought and spread out just beyond the edge of the stream. As they ate, the conversation was general, mostly about Melanie and her family and the one trip they had all made to the mountains together. That had been before her parents had bought the cabin. The family had camped on the far side of the cabin, in a public campground. She told Mac several anecdotes about camping with a family of six.

"I remember going fishing in this stream when we were all up here. There was no way any fish would have bitten with the racket we were making. But my dad just acted like everything was exactly as it was supposed to be.

"My mom sat on the bank and laughed at us. Liane was mooning about Chuck the whole time, and Clay and Jeremy were trying to see who could get the wettest. But not me."

As she gazed out at the stream, she felt Mac squeeze her hand.

"You wanted to catch a fish."

She looked at him in surprise. "Yes, I did. I really wanted to show my dad that I could do it. And I did. I caught a fish. Then I cried so hard after I caught it that they put it back just to shut me up."

He had fallen strangely silent, and Melanie mentally kicked herself for bringing up happy childhood memories of her own when Mac couldn't remember last week.

After they had eaten and cleared away the trash and placed it in public receptacles, Melanie sat on the grass in the shade and leaned against a tree trunk, pulling at grass blades and chewing on them. Mac sat next to her, then stretched out on the ground with his head on her lap and fell asleep. Melanie wasn't sure if he had intended to fall asleep or not, but she didn't mind. She sat quietly and watched him. He looked so innocent, so uncomplicated in sleep, but she knew that when he woke, his intelligent mind would return to its investigation of his lost self.

She lightly stroked his smooth brow and wondered what he had been like as a child. How had he gotten the tiny scar at the corner of his left eye? What were his political opinions? His feelings about the environment and the arts? Did he ever want children? Melanie rolled her eyes.

She was afraid that in her desire for him she had begun to project onto him the traits she would like him to have before she found out what he really was like.

She wondered how their relationship might have grown if it had been allowed to follow a normal path. Would he have wanted a relationship with her after the one date they were to have had together?

Melanie wished that they had been able to have that date. Then, at least, she would have been able to have known a little about what he was like before now. She prayed he wouldn't change. She was in love with this man: the one with whom she had spent the last three days. They had hardly been separated in that time, and she was afraid that he might not feel the same toward her when he regained his memory.

A sudden thought stuck through to her consciousness. How did Mac feel? This Mac? The one who had shown her so much passion and tenderness? The one who had trusted her judgment and let her take him to a cabin hideout? She didn't know how he felt about her. Maybe he was just enjoying what had been offered to him while he was waiting for his memory to return. Maybe he didn't feel anything close to what she felt for him so soon after meeting. How could he? She vowed to keep her emotions under control until he gave her some indication as to how he felt. She had already told him she was falling in love with him. What more was there to tell? A lot, she told herself. Mac stirred and opened his eyes.

"Oh, I guess I must have fallen asleep." He stretched, but didn't give any indication he intended to remove his head from her lap.

She smiled. "My father used to claim he was just resting his eyes," she reminisced, her eyes misting with tears at the memory. Mac sat up slowly and brushed a strand of hair from her cheek. He kissed her on the tip of her nose and then rose, bringing her with him. They picked up their packs, which were somewhat lighter, and started back along the trail toward the cabin in a companionable silence, stopping occasionally to watch a wild animal through the trees or to drink from the stream.

After they had returned to the cabin and put away the remains of their lunch, Melanie suggested they go berry picking and pulled two small buckets from under the sink. Mac followed her out the door, and they spent several hours picking and eating berries. When they finally returned to the cabin they only had one of the buckets half-filled with berries.

Mac began making noises about dinner, and after she made a few remarks about bottomless pits disguised as stomachs, Melanie suggested they go fishing off the dock on the small lake about two hundred yards behind the cabin. Mac helped her search the house for the gear she knew would be there. They found it in the kitchen closet.

They set off down the trail behind the cabin and reached the lake in less than five minutes. They sat down on the weather-beaten dock and hung their hooks in the water. After twenty minutes of quiet fishing jokes and no fish, Mac stood up.

"I think we're too close to the edge of the water," he announced, and began looking around.

"That very well may be," Melanie agreed. "But how do we get out into the middle of the lake without a boat?"

"What is that?" he asked, pointing to a clump of weeds. Melanie peered at the weeds.

"That, Wendell, is a clump of weeds."

He shot her a withering glance at her use of his first name, and strode over to the weeds. "There's a boat in here," he called.

Melanie laid her pole on the dock and stood up, trying to see through the weeds. "Well, even if there is, it would hardly be seaworthy. Or even puddleworthy."

He ignored her remarks and began pulling at the ancient canoe. Melanie took pity on him and went over to help him. When it sank as it hit the water, he would give up, she decided. But after they had dragged the canoe to the water's edge and slid its paint-peeled hull into the water, it didn't sink. It didn't look safe, either. Melanie looked doubtfully at the canoe while Mac loaded it with their fishing gear.

"Uh, Mac," she began casually, "have you run across anything that resembles a paddle?"

"Paddle?" His brows came together, and he looked back to where they had found the canoe. Melanie felt a wave of laughter hit her and fought to keep it under control. Mac looked so serious. He turned just as she clapped a hand over her mouth to stifle the rising giggle.

"You don't think it's *funny* do you?" He took a threatening step toward her. She pulled her hand away from her face and shook her head, not trusting her voice to hide the laughter.

"Good," he said. "Anyway, we don't need paddles. It's just a little lake. We'll paddle with our hands."

Melanie started laughing and backing up as he came toward her.

"Okay," she said, putting her hands up in a surrender. "We'll paddle with our hands." When Mac had turned to get into the canoe, she added, "But I hope you can swim."

"What was that crack?"

"Oh, nothing, Skipper, nothing at all. Ready to cast off."

Melanie wasn't aware that Mac had taken a particular notice of her little jibes, but as she stepped into the boat he grabbed her around the waist and hauled her down onto his lap.

"I believe mutiny is punishable by death?"

Melanie stared wide-eyed at him. "Couldn't I just die from ecstasy instead?"

"Your last wish is my command," he said softly just before his lips took hers.

Melanie felt desire course through her. She had felt the power of Mac's kisses before, but now . . . there was something more now. Something more urgent. It was like a hunger, and she gave herself over to it without thinking.

His hands moved over her back, and her fingers dug into the muscles of his shoulders. She trembled when she felt his lips leave hers and trail over to her ear. Her stomach clenched, and her breath became trapped in her throat.

When she attempted to speak, all that came from her lips was a gasp and a moan. Melanie never found out what she might have said if she'd found her voice, for it was then that they suddenly felt the canoe lurch beneath them.

"Ohh, Mac!" Melanie cried as she felt the bow of the canoe dip into the water under their weight. She scrambled off his lap to the other side of the canoe. Mac began paddling with his arms, and Melanie took his cue. The wild abandon of their kisses was put aside as they struggled to propel the canoe without swamping it. Melanie was glad no one else was out on the lake, because they looked rather ridiculous. Fortunately, it took them only a few minutes to get to the middle of the lake.

"See?" Mac pulled out the fishing gear, obviously feeling very proud of himself and his little maneuver. Melanie smiled to herself and put her unbaited hook over the edge of the canoe. The sun was beginning to dip behind the

SILHOUETTE DELIVERS FIRST-CLASS ROMANCE— DIRECT TO YOUR DOOR

Mail the Heart sticker on the postpaid order card today and you'll receive:

—4 new Silhouette Romance™ novels—FREE
—a lovely lucite digital clock/calendar—FREE
—and a surprise mystery bonus—FREE

But that's not all. You'll also get:

Free Home Delivery

When you subscribe to Silhouette Romance™, the excitement, romance and faraway adventures of these novels can be yours for previewing in the convenience of your own home. Every month we'll deliver 6 new books right to your door. If you decide to keep them, they'll be yours for only $2.25* each, and there is *no* extra charge for postage and handling! There is no obligation to buy—you can cancel at any time simply by writing ''cancel'' on your statement or by returning a shipment of books to us at our cost.

Free Monthly Newsletter

It's the indispensable insider's look at our most popular writers and their upcoming novels. Now you can have a behind-the-scenes look at the fascinating world of Silhouette! It's an added bonus you'll look forward to every month!

Special Extras—FREE

Because our home subscribers are our most valued readers, we'll be sending you additional free gifts from time to time in your monthly book shipments as a token of our appreciation.

OPEN YOUR MAILBOX TO A WORLD OF LOVE AND ROMANCE EACH MONTH. JUST COMPLETE, DETACH AND MAIL YOUR FREE-OFFER CARD TODAY!

FREE! lucite digital clock/calendar

You'll love your digital clock/calendar!
The changeable month-at-a-glance calendar
pops out and can be replaced with your
favorite photograph. It is yours FREE as
our gift of love!

FREE OFFER CARD

4 FREE BOOKS

FREE DIGITAL CLOCK/CALENDAR

FREE MYSTERY BONUS

PLACE HEART STICKER HERE

FREE HOME DELIVERY

FREE FACT-FILLED NEWSLETTER

MORE SURPRISES THROUGHOUT THE YEAR—FREE

✓ **YES!** Please send me four Silhouette Romance™ novels, free, along with my free digital clock/ calendar and my free mystery gift as explained on the opposite page.

215 CIS HAYE
(U-S-R-11/89)

NAME _____

ADDRESS _____ APT. _____

CITY _____ STATE _____

ZIP CODE _____

Offer limited to one per household and not valid to current Silhouette Romance subscribers. All orders subject to approval. Terms and prices subject to change without notice.

MAIL THE POSTPAID CARD TODAY!

Remember! To receive your free books, digital clock/calendar and mystery gift, return the postpaid card below. But don't delay!

DETACH AND MAIL CARD TODAY.

MAIL THE POSTPAID CARD TODAY!

BUSINESS REPLY CARD

FIRST CLASS MAIL   PERMIT NO. 717   BUFFALO, NY

POSTAGE WILL BE PAID BY ADDRESSEE

SILHOUETTE BOOKS
901 FUHRMANN BLVD
PO BOX 1867
BUFFALO NY 14240-9952

NO POSTAGE
NECESSARY
IF MAILED
IN THE
UNITED STATES

mountains, and Melanie guessed it was around seven o'clock. It would be another hour and a half before it was totally dark out, and she was happy just to sit and enjoy the changing colors of the Oregon sky.

Mac caught two small fish and let them both go, much to Melanie's relief. Seeing those poor fish flop around in the bottom of the canoe was a reminder as to why she had become a vegetarian. She only went fishing as an excuse to enjoy the scenery in peace and to listen to sounds of the wilderness. Mac seemed to be comfortable with their shared silence, and Melanie sighed in contentment.

The shadows were lengthening, and it was becoming difficult to see distances when Melanie discovered something was wrong. She moved her feet to reach her pole and heard the slosh. Water?

She looked down and saw that the canoe had at least an inch of water in its bottom. She carefully laid her pole along the seats at the edge of the canoe and watched as the water soaked her tennis shoes. Not much to be done. She looked down at Mac's feet and saw that he was wearing his hiking boots, the only footwear available to him other than his dress shoes. He wouldn't notice the water until it was two or three inches deep, unless he happened to look down.

Melanie leaned forward and rested her chin on his right shoulder. He snuggled against her for a moment, and she smiled. What a guy. She put her hand on his back and rubbed it before saying, "Mac, guess what?"

"Hmm?"

"We seem to have acquired a somewhat less-than-waterproof vessel."

Mac jerked upright and stared at the water that was steadily pouring into the little boat from some unknown source. "Damn," he said, pulling off his hiking boots and placing them carefully on the forward bow seat. "These boots were custom-made."

Melanie laughed as he proceeded to strip off his shirt and socks but stopped when he started on his jeans. "You're serious!" she cried. "What are you going to do? Tow the canoe to the dock?"

Mac folded his clothes and placed them on the seat next to his boots. "That's right."

She stared at him dumbly. She was staring at a crazy man in his underwear. She tried to concentrate on his mental deficiencies instead of his physical attributes, which were pretty obvious to her now. A crazy man. That's what he was. She was on a lake at sundown with a crazy man. "Mac, there's no rope."

"I know. I'm going to swim to the dock and get one. I suggest you swim to shore now, yourself, because as much as I admire and adore your body, I'm not going to haul it with the canoe." With that he eased himself over the side of the canoe and struck out for the dock. Melanie debated only a moment before taking off her wet tennis shoes. Not that they were custom-made and worth saving, but it would be easier to swim—

She suddenly stared at her tennis shoes, then looked over at Mac's boots. Custom-made? He'd remembered something else! She wondered if he was even aware of it. She looked up just as he dove back into the lake from the dock, a piece of rope in hand.

As she stripped down to her underwear, she looked around the lake. No one for miles. She waited anxiously for Mac to return, debating with herself over whether or not she should mention his boots. Would it be better to let him realize it on his own, or should she tell him and see if it helped bring back more?

She was still contemplating this when she helped him tie the rope to the metal hook on the bow of the canoe before easing herself over the edge and into the water. Now was probably not the best time, she decided. The man was towing a canoe across a lake. He needed his concentration.

She swam slowly and leisurely, turning frequently to tread water and watch Mac doing the side stroke, pulling his burden. Maybe a subtle hint wouldn't be out of place, she thought. Turning, she laughed and said, "All this for a pair of boots?" When he just grunted, she sighed and turned, swimming the remaining twenty feet to the dock. She grasped the dock and pulled herself up.

The warm air cooled on her wet skin, and her lacy underwear plastered itself to her body. Melanie thought that she might as well not have been wearing anything at all.

Mac pulled the canoe under the dock and tied it. He gathered their clothes and the fishing gear and placed them on the dock next to Melanie. Then he pulled himself up onto the dock and shook the lake water out of his hair. He was breathing heavily, but was not overexerted.

"Whew! I guess we'll have to waterproof that thing before we go out again."

Again. The word echoed in Melanie's mind. He acted as if he planned to return. Melanie suddenly felt uncomfortable. If she was right, he was very close to regaining his memory. Would he really want to return here with her? She didn't even have an idea about what Mac felt toward her—other than what was obvious as he looked at her nearly naked body. She shivered suddenly, and it wasn't from being cold.

What right did she have to expect him to return feelings that she knew had been growing since she had first seen him? She was beginning to believe that they were meant for each other, but was it enough for her to know that? Didn't he have to feel the same way? Her doubts about their bizarre relationship surfaced, and she wondered if she had made the biggest mistake of her life.

The mistake wasn't in helping him, but in giving her heart to someone who could very well not want it.

Not noticing Mac pulling the canoe onto the shore, Melanie shivered again and gazed worriedly at the graying horizon over the mountains. Maybe he didn't know how he felt. That thought only made her feel worse. If she knew how she felt, why shouldn't he know how he felt?

Telling herself she was stupid for getting involved with an amnesia victim and then expecting him to know his own mind, she warned herself not to pass judgment. But she couldn't shrug off her doubts and insecurities. She bent and picked up her clothes, leaving Mac staring after her as she started off for the cabin.

She could feel his eyes on her as they walked. She felt naked and vulnerable, but she kept her back straight and tried to ignore the feeling that he was touching her with his eyes. She stepped carefully around a tree root and saw the cabin through the haze of twilight.

She pulled the door open and entered the dark cabin. Without stopping, she headed for the bedroom, where she dug out fresh underwear, then put her shorts and top back on. She was considering staying in the bedroom when the door was suddenly flung open.

"What is wrong?" he demanded.

"Nothing," she answered quietly, hoping he couldn't see her confusion.

He reached out and grabbed her wrist, pulling her into the living room. She noticed that he had put on his jeans and lit several candles. His chest was still bare, and Melanie frowned at it, thinking that he shouldn't look so good when she was trying to control her emotions. He took a candle and put it on the coffee table with a controlled precision that made Melanie wonder if he was angry. Then he grasped both her shoulders and said, "Melanie, I know something is wrong. Tell me what it is."

She shivered again suddenly and realized vaguely that she was covered with goose bumps. "I'm cold." She hoped to avoid a crying scene, especially since she knew who would be doing all the crying.

He released her, and she swayed away from him. He reached over to the back of the couch and pulled off the crocheted afghan and wrapped it around her, pulling her back to him as he did it.

"Now, will you tell me what is wrong?"

Melanie felt her head clear, and she took a deep breath. Knowing she might be pushing him too much before he was ready for it, she met his gaze directly and said, "Mac, I know you haven't gotten your memory back." She saw his eyes drop briefly, then return to meet hers. "But, I have to know how you feel about me. This you, the you that I know. I've told you how I feel, but I don't know how you feel about me."

Mac paused for a second that felt like an eternity to Melanie. Then he bent his head so that his forehead rested on hers, and their noses touched. He kissed her warmly and sighed.

"Of course, you know how I feel, darling." *Darling?* "I'm crazy about you." He kissed her again, and she suddenly threw her arms around his neck and kissed him back. Then she pulled away and whispered, "But you might feel differently when you get your memory back."

He pulled her back into his embrace, and she rested her head on his chest, under his chin. "Regaining my memory doesn't mean I have to forget the present." He let go of the afghan and grasped her head, his thumbs caressing her jawline.

His lips lowered to hers, and he kissed her with a tenderness that brought tears to her eyes. "Oh, Mac," she gasped when he released her mouth to concentrate on her neck. "I can't believe that I didn't even know you a few days ago."

Mac groaned as he kissed his way back to her lips. "Even without my memory I felt as if I'd known you forever."

Not noticing the change of tense, Melanie kissed his jaw and said, "What a sweet thing to say."

"You like that?"

"Yes, it's almost poetic. Much better than 'get out and swim because I'm only saving my boots.'"

He laughed. "I would have saved you, too, but you had already told me you knew how to swim."

She smiled and decided to tell him that he'd remembered something else, when she realized he had spoken of his memory loss in the past tense. The smile slid from her lips as she stepped away from him and looked into his eyes. Her words were deceptively calm.

"How long have you had your memory back?"

She waited for his eyes to close or look away, but they didn't. They narrowed a bit, then widened in honesty. "Since this morning."

Chapter Seven

She couldn't remember how long she stood and stared at Mac. He remained silent, his eyes never leaving her face. Finally, she realized she was trembling, and she shook her head, trying to clear it.

"Why..." she began, and found that she couldn't speak because of a huge lump in her throat. Her brain had gone numb of every thought but one: Mac had lied to her. The Mac she was falling in love with was gone. Her fears had proved valid. Her lips trembled as she struggled for control. Her carefully constructed, emotionally frail world was crumbling. Melanie was afraid of crumbling with it. She cleared her throat.

"Why did you wait so long to tell me?"

As he started to speak, she held up a hand. "No, wait. I've got that wrong. You didn't tell me. I figured it out for myself."

Mac reached out a hand to touch her shoulder, but Melanie flinched and backed up a step. "No," she said, closing her eyes, not seeing the expression of frustration on his face. "No, don't. I don't think that is such a good idea. I'm borderline right now, and not doing too well in the self-control department."

"Are you at least going to let me explain?" He sounded calm but determined. Melanie stared into the black depths of the eyes she had come to know so well and started to shake her head. She didn't know if she wanted to listen to him any more right now. It would be too easy for her to give in to his charisma. He had power over her. She had given him far too much of herself, and now he had her in his power. Her hurt was too raw to withstand his excuses, but she needed to know the reason for his deception.

"All I want to know is why you didn't tell me when it happened."

Mac took a deep breath and let it out slowly. "I was still so confused, Melanie. You have to believe that. I wanted to sort out everything for myself, without any help. It didn't all come back in an instant, you know. It came in bits and pieces all day."

Melanie considered this and asked, "What was it that triggered your memory?"

Mac smiled that smile, and Melanie wondered how she could still love him when he had treated her this way.

"It was something you said."

Something she said? Melanie ran back over the events of the day, trying to remember something she had said that could have signaled the return of his lost memory, but she couldn't remember anything outstanding. When she simply shook her head and looked at him questioningly, he hooked a thumb in a belt loop of his jeans, and Melanie couldn't stop her gaze from drifting to his bare stomach. She suddenly felt hot and threw the afghan off, not caring that it fell to the floor in a forgotten heap. Mac cleared his throat, and she jerked her gaze back to his face. He seemed amused about something, and Melanie was afraid it was her.

"It was when we were hiking. Remember when I wanted to stop for lunch?" Melanie nodded.

Mac moved away then, calmly walking around the room, lighting more candles. "I sat down, but you wanted to move on. Do you remember what you said to me?"

Melanie's mind raced back to that moment. She had laughed at him and said something like—

He completed her thought verbally. "You said, 'On your feet, soldier.'"

Melanie nodded and followed his movements around the room with her eyes. He seemed so at ease. Shouldn't he be shifting from foot to foot under the guilt of his sin? He didn't look as though he felt very guilty. In fact, he looked suspiciously confident.

"When you said that, I suddenly saw a 'flash from the past' as they say. I was in the army for eight years."

Her mouth dropped open. Her jesting remark had hit the mark and led to the recovery of his memory. She tried to make her lips move to form words, but her voice wouldn't cooperate.

"From that point on," he was continuing, "the pieces just sort of floated into place."

Melanie felt like an outsider. He still hadn't explained why he hadn't told her. Maybe he hadn't wanted to. Maybe he had felt uncomfortable about the intensity of the relationship he had formed with a stranger. Melanie abruptly sat down, since her legs wouldn't support her.

She wet her lips and asked, "So, when did all the pieces form the whole picture?"

His eyes narrowed slightly as he looked at her, and he spoke carefully.

"During the time we spent picking berries and fishing."

Melanie felt cold again. Not on the outside but on the inside.

"Were you ever going to tell me? Or were you simply going to let me go on making a fool of myself until we got back to Bayview, where you would, no doubt, dump me at my doorstep and go back to Salem?"

She was practically shouting by the time she stopped to catch her breath. Mac stood by the fireplace, a stunned expression on his face. He took a step toward her.

"Melanie, how could you say that after everything—"

"I can say it because it's true. Isn't it?" she demanded. He stepped closer to her and grabbed her by the shoulders, shaking her slightly.

"Melanie, sweetheart, you aren't thinking straight."

She wrenched away and took refuge at the other end of the couch. "Of course, I'm thinking straight—and don't call me sweetheart. You lied to me. You probably lied about everything else, too."

"What?" He sounded incredulous. "Melanie, you aren't being fair. You can't mean this. You're making this whole weekend sound like a bad dream."

She tilted her chin upward. "Don't worry, Mac, your nightmare will soon be over. I'm going to pack, and then we'll go back to Bayview. We never have to see each other again."

"That's what you think." His nostrils flared as he struggled for composure, and slowly approached her. "You're not going to run away from me, Melanie. From us."

Before she thought to move, his strong fingers closed around her shoulders and he brought her to her feet.

"Us?" she cried, trying to pull away from his iron grip. She grasped his forearms and felt the tensed muscles, knowing she couldn't push him away. She wanted to lash out at him because she was hurt and she was mad—and because she felt betrayed. Her only weapon was words.

"There is no 'us.' There is you, who obviously didn't care enough to tell me something very important about yourself, and there is me, the dumb jerk who tried to be your protector. I'll bet that gave you a laugh."

Mac suddenly released her, and she stumbled a step backward. She swayed slightly, but managed to regain her balance. Her gaze, however, never wavered from his face. Mac was staring at her in disbelief.

"I can't believe you said that!"

Neither of them heard the knock on the door of the cabin.

"Why not? It's true."

"You didn't act like a 'protector' in that boat a while ago!" he yelled at her. Melanie paled. It was as if he had slapped her. He was demeaning everything they had shared.

"Well," she said evenly, fighting the tears that threatened to spill down her cheeks, "I guess that just proves how really naive and gullible I am, doesn't it? I'll just chalk this catastrophe up to experience and hope I have more sense with men in future. My lack of experience is probably what got me into this mess to begin with. Well, you can be sure of one thing, Wendell Chandler," she shouted at him, "I won't be so stupid as to let a pretty face and great body delude me again. The next time I get involved with a man—"

"The hell you will!" he roared. "If you ever even look at another man that way, I'll break your neck!"

"Why should you care?" she screamed back at him. "Why don't you just go now? Go back to Nancy's and get into that black Jaguar of yours—which, incidentally, you wouldn't even have if it wasn't for me—and just go back to Salem and leave me alone!"

"No, I won't!"

"Why not?"

"Because now I have to protect you until this is over."

Melanie wasn't sure if she should be happy because he wanted to protect her or sad because that protectiveness was all he felt for her. Tears sprang to her eyes and began slowly rolling down her cheeks.

"Oh, Melanie, don't cry. Come on, that's not fair."

She felt herself weakening, and then remembered why they had been fighting. She sniffed loudly and drew herself up. "You still haven't told me why you didn't tell me you'd gotten your memory back."

He raked his fingers through his hair and massaged the back of his neck. "Melanie, I swear, I was just waiting for the—"

"Oh, don't tell me," she said, waving her hand in his face. "You were waiting for the right time."

When he nodded curtly, she took a deep breath.

"Mac, didn't you think that letting me believe you still couldn't remember anything was like lying to me? And you let me go on about how I feel about you. What were you doing? Testing me?"

He flinched and took a step backward. "Of course not. I hope you don't believe that."

"Why shouldn't I? What would you think if the situation had been reversed?"

He pointed an accusing finger at her. "I hope I would believe you when you said that you cared about me and forgive me for my error in judgment. I'm not sorry I kissed you just now, so if you think I'm going to apologize for it, you can just forget it. And you enjoyed it just as much as I did!"

Melanie gasped and took a step forward to shove her finger under Mac's nose. "How dare you say that to me! After what I went through for you. Not to mention your stupid car!"

"Exactly how *did* you get my Jag back that night?"

Melanie gaped at him. How dare he worry about that hunk of metal? And she had done it all for him, the ingrate!

"I bribed a cab driver, snuck around the square and eluded two killers as I drove it back to Lansport."

He paled. "You drove my Jag?"

"Yes, I did," she shot back. "And I ground so many gears that it's a wonder your transmission didn't fall out on the highway!"

It was then that they heard the laughter. And the quiet, rhythmic knocking. They stared at each other, then Mac quickly strode to the door and pulled it open.

A man was leaning on the doorway, chuckling to himself and examining his knuckles.

"It's about time," the man said. "I have been knocking for five minutes straight. My knuckles are raw."

Mac was stupefied. "Kyle?"

His brother! Melanie had forgotten she had told him to come up. Nancy was just behind him, looking deceptively innocent.

"That's me," he said easily, moving into the living room. "Glad to see the memory's back. The case is getting a little sticky, if you know what I mean."

He looked pointedly at Melanie, then at Mac. When they both remained silent, he put out his hand and took Melanie's, which was hanging limply at her side, and shook it warmly.

"You must be Melanie. I'm Kyle. Our voices met on my recorder, but it's so much nicer in person, don't you think?"

She nodded dumbly, and he smiled. Then he dropped her hand and folded his arms over his chest and let out a soft whistle, looking at Nancy, who still stood in the doorway. "Maybe we should go back outside and let these two finish their, er, altercation?"

Melanie felt her face turn red. They had heard everything, or practically everything. She had never been so embarrassed. Not because of Nancy, but Kyle! These two now knew everything there was to know about Mac and her. She spared a look at Mac, but he was staring at his brother as if he were an alien. Then Kyle spoke again.

"Did you really grind the gears of his Jag?" When she nodded, he laughed. "Did you peel out and leave a little rubber?" Again she nodded, and Kyle laughed outright. "God, I wish I'd been there! He won't even let me drive it around the block."

Melanie felt herself relaxing, the tension seeping out of her muscles.

"You know," Kyle said, "I know you both can talk because I was out on that porch listening to you while I knocked my knuckles red."

"Why didn't you knock louder?" Mac asked his brother.

Kyle shrugged. "What, and miss the good parts?" He looked at Melanie again with a smile of genuine humor and a bit of respect.

"You really shouldn't call him Wendell, though. I can't tell you the number of beatings I received for mentioning his inherited first name. Did he tell you about dear old Uncle Wendell who died and left him a bundle? Mom and Dad knew what they were doing."

Melanie suddenly wanted to get away from Mac and his brother. Her nerves were still too raw for casual conversation.

"Pardon me, Kyle, but since you're here, I'm going to pack. Perhaps we can talk again later."

Shooting a look at Nancy, she whirled and stomped off to the bedroom, waiting until Nancy had entered the room, then slamming the door behind them, although without the force that she had felt capable of earlier. She sagged against the door, but jumped when she heard Mac's voice on the other side.

"Melanie? Don't think I'm going to let this go so easily. We will talk."

She stared at the door and muttered, "Oh, go talk to your brother."

She heard his steps retreat and sighed with relief. She walked over to the bed and sank onto it, burying her face in her hands, sighing raggedly. Nancy watched her, waiting for permission to speak.

Melanie straightened after a minute and took a deep breath. Looking morosely at her sodden tennis shoes, she wondered what she was going to put on her feet. She sighed again and forced herself to look at Nancy, who stood leaning against the door.

"What?"

An eyebrow arched upward. "I didn't say anything."

"No, but you were thinking it."

"What was I thinking?"

Melanie crossed her arms over her chest. "That I was a sap to fall for that big oaf."

"Is that what I was thinking?" Nancy mused. "And here I was thinking that I was thinking how happy I was for you that you were in love."

Melanie's jaw was set stubbornly as she glared at her friend. "Don't be happy. Feel sorry for me. Besides, it's probably just a crush. If I'm lucky."

"Nope. I think it's love. And I think he loves you, too."

Melanie was about to protest, when she heard Kyle's voice through the door.

"Well, well, big brother," Kyle said as Melanie and Nancy shamelessly eavesdropped, "it would appear as though you have got it bad. But in your case maybe that's good."

"Oh, shut up," Mac retorted. Melanie tried to tell herself that eavesdroppers heard nothing good, but found that she was perversely straining to hear their conversation.

"Ooh," Kyle mocked. "It would appear that we are a might sensitive on the subject." Then his voice became serious. "Do you want to talk about it?"

Mac murmured something Melanie couldn't hear, and she found herself dying of curiosity about what he had told his brother. She glanced at Nancy, who had moved away from the door. They were talking about her, so didn't she have a right to hear? She crept back to the door, waited, and Kyle spoke again.

"Well, if you don't want her, I'd be more than willing to—" Nancy flew back to where Melanie stood by the door, pressing her ear to the wood.

His voice trailed off, and Melanie began to boil. "What do they think I am, a head of cattle?" she whispered furiously. She didn't hear Mac say anything, but then she heard Kyle's voice. He sounded amused.

"Hey, you're really serious aren't you? I was wondering if you would ever fall, and here you are—"

"Didn't I tell you shut up?"

"Defensive, too. Liz is not going to like this. She's been telling people you two are still together. But this...Melanie's nothing like Liz. Wait until I tell Mom. When's the wedding?"

Melanie sucked her breath in. Who was Liz? She could feel the tears starting. She realized that she didn't want to hear what Mac was about to say. She backed away from the door. She was half praying that he would prove her wrong when she heard him responding to his brother's jest.

"Who said anything about marriage? I only met Melanie four days ago, and as you can testify, we are currently having a difference of opinion."

Melanie sank onto the bed, tears rolling down her cheeks. She had been right. Nancy came and sat next to her, putting her arm around Melanie's shoulders.

"I don't think he really means that, Mel."

Melanie appreciated Nancy's attempts to reassure her, but didn't think she was right. She could still hear their voices, but it didn't seem to matter anymore.

"I heard a lot of things, Mac. But if you want to talk about it some other time, I understand. We do have to talk about this WilCom business, though."

Melanie didn't hear anything after that. She let Nancy gather up her clothes and pack them, and her friend talked quietly with her and listened when she babbled that it didn't matter, that she had known it wouldn't last from the beginning and that she would be better off with someone who didn't cause her to experience such overwhelming emotional highs and lows. She had been happy and content before last week, hadn't she? She would be again. It was simply a matter of getting back to Bayview and returning to her life.

Even as she tried to convince Nancy, she was really trying to convince herself, and Melanie knew that nothing would ever be the same. Her feelings for Mac were new and fragile, but they were there, inside her heart, and she knew she would never find another man like Mac. She never wanted to. But she also didn't want it to be over like this. She felt helpless and quite vulnerable. She walked to the window and stared into the darkness, hardly noticing when Nancy slipped from the room.

Melanie grumbled and made several self-deprecating remarks as she forced herself away from the window and to the door. After wiping her eyes, she opened the door cautiously. No one was in the living room. She was suddenly afraid that Mac had left her there with no explanation and no goodbye. She practically ran over to the window and looked out. She breathed an audible sigh of relief when she saw the Mazda sitting in the drive.

"Afraid I'd left?"

Mac's voice came from behind her, and Melanie whirled around to face him. He had finished dressing and had been outside gathering wood to replace what they had used. She stared at him for a moment and then found her voice.

"Where are Kyle and Nancy?"

Mac deposited the wood in the box next to the fireplace and returned to stand in front of her. "They just left. We're following as soon as we load the car. Kyle and I have closed the place up."

So, Melanie thought, *he can't wait to get rid of me.*

"Don't you dare get that look, Melanie," he warned.

Her gaze swung to face him. He looked rather formidable.

"What do you mean?"

He drew his brows together. "You know what I mean. That martyr look. We have a lot to talk about, Melanie, but we'll do it in the car on the way back because this WilCom thing is coming to a head and I have to get back and finish it up."

Melanie looked at the repacked bag of groceries sitting on the table. She dug an apple out, bit into it and then said, "What's going on at WilCom?"

Mac sighed. "Just forget it, Melanie. It involves some top-secret government information, and the less you know the better off you'll be."

Melanie's jaw dropped. Top secret? That wasn't what Liane had told her. "I thought you were hired by WilCom for some computer evaluation."

Mac shook his head. "That was a cover. Now, don't ask. As it is, I'm going to have to see if I can have you placed in protective custody."

"Protective custody!" Melanie screeched. "No way. And you can't just say something like that and not expect me to ask about it," she said. "I may have been better off if I'd never gotten involved, but it's too late for that. I have already—''

''I don't want you to get involved any further,'' he stated flatly.

Melanie was beginning to feel like an unruly child instead of a responsible adult. ''Look, Mac, I think that I have proven myself capable of keeping a secret. And, unless I'm mistaken, I have probably seen and heard far more than I would normally have been allowed. I think I deserve to know what is going on.''

He gazed at her for a minute. ''All right,'' he said finally. ''I should have known you wouldn't agree to be taken into protective custody. You're right, by the way, you've seen too much. That causes a certain number of problems.''

''What problems?''

He raised his gaze to the ceiling. ''Problems like how to protect you now that those men have seen you. Like the fact that they think you're in this with me. They know who you are, Melanie...Kyle said that your apartment had been ransacked.''

When she shook her head to clear it, Mac groaned. ''I'm sorry I had to tell you that, but you had to know. You'll have to stay with me and Kyle. Nancy's agreed to let us use her house as a base until the unit arrives. Just so you know, Kyle ran a check on you after he got your message. He was concerned because you're a journalist, but he said you weren't a threat.''

When she stared at him with huge hazel eyes in amazement, Mac sighed. ''Of course, he's never spent any time with you, either.''

He shook his head resignedly and carried their bags to the front door. ''Come on. I'll tell you about it on the way back.''

Once in the car, he watched her face for signs of fear, but Melanie was too numb to show any emotion at all. She just sat there with her hands clenched in front of her, waiting for him to continue.

"I wasn't hired by Frank Wilson to reevaluate his computer-programming department," he stated. "I was hired by the government to investigate the possibility that someone has been using one of their computer systems for espionage."

Melanie's mouth was already hanging open, but her eyes grew as large as saucers as she stared at him.

He casually put out a finger and closed her gaping mouth for her. That action stirred her brain, and she blurted out the first thing that popped into her mind.

"Are you with the CIA or the FBI or—"

"No, I am not," he interrupted. "Kyle is, though. FBI."

"I am...a private computer consultant." He frowned for a moment, considering her expression. Then, "I was hired independently."

"Wait a minute," Melanie said, trying to make sense of this. "Obviously, the government wouldn't have hired you without a reason. Why you?"

He paused a moment, seeming to choose his words carefully. "When I was in the army, I was part of a team of computer and engineering specialists who put together a satellite communications program. WilCom supplied the hardware and some of the software for the project."

"When did you get out of the army?"

He hesitated briefly, then looked away. "Nine months ago."

Melanie thought that he seemed to be telling her the bare minimum of facts. This didn't surprise her too much, considering their weird association. His unwillingness to be straight with her only made her push harder for the truth.

"Why did you leave?"

He seemed slightly taken aback by her question. She had already figured out that Mac did nothing halfway—even when he had had amnesia—so she doubted that he had spent eight years in the army for nothing. Nor did she think he had just left on a whim.

"Why do you ask?" He was hedging, and she chewed her cheek for a moment. Maybe it was none of her business. If he didn't want to tell her about himself and his past, then she would be better off just shutting up and leaving him alone. It was curiosity versus his right to privacy. Curiosity won because she felt that she had a stake in the outcome of this madness.

"Mac, I know we haven't known each other very long . . . but let me take a few guesses at your previously un-revealed past. You were an officer in the army, I'll bet." At his mildly surprised nod, she continued. "That means you either went to West Point or you went to college and had ROTC or you're a ninety-day wonder who whizzed through officer's candidate school."

"How do you know all that military—"

She waved a hand dismissingly and said, "One of my brothers was in the navy. Now, let me think." She pretended to size him up. "I don't think you went to West Point."

"Why not?"

"Because you aren't regimented enough. You leave your socks on the floor and wet towels in the bathroom."

He laughed at her insight and encouraged her to go on.

"Neither do I think that you were a ninety-day wonder. You're more of a planner than that. And from what my brother has said, they are a reckless crew. No, I think you went ROTC."

Mac was smiling now. "Oh, don't stop now, you're on a roll."

She nodded slightly and looked out the window while she formulated her ideas. She tapped her finger on the dash and then turned and pointed it at him.

"I don't know where you went to school," she reasoned out loud, "but I'd be willing to bet a large sum of money—if I had any—that it was someplace like Stanford or Cal Tech or MIT or some other equally distinguished institution of higher learning for the academically gifted."

"Thanks, I think," was his only reply. Melanie wavered for a moment. What if she were on the wrong track? No, she was more than just guessing, and judging from the look on Mac's face, she was more right than wrong. So she continued.

"I think you probably got some outrageously high scores on your college board exams, and every college you applied to and some you didn't offered you all kinds of scholarships, but you had already made up your mind." She paused and looked at him, suddenly aware that the anger she had felt earlier was a pale memory. Mac looked back thoughtfully, an unreadable expression on his handsome features.

"Oh, please go on," he said, his voice low and thoughtful. She nodded and leaned back.

"I don't know why you chose the military—family ties, personal reasons, whatever—you went to college and got one, maybe two, degrees in computer science or math or whatever and then you went into the army, and you were working on highly sensitive stuff. Now—" she took a deep breath as she wound down her attempted life story "—I am prone to think you were planning on the military as a career, but something—or someone—messed it up. So, you left and started your own company, and now the army still has your number. And you have theirs."

She finished and waited for him to confirm or deny her guesswork. He was watching the road and her, an enigmatic gleam in his dark eyes.

"Well?" Melanie asked finally. "How'd I do?"

Mac turned his head and smiled. "Actually, you were very nearly perfect. But then, I already knew that."

Despite her attempt at self-control, Melanie felt herself swell with pleasure and blush slightly. How would she ever be able to get over him? That thought sobered her as no other could. Mac wasn't interested in a serious commitment. He had made that clear in his remarks to his brother. And since Melanie couldn't see herself having a casual, dead-end affair—in spite of how quickly and deeply she had gotten involved with Mac—she didn't see much future for them.

"I went to Cal Tech, and I got two degrees in Computational Mathematics. I had already planned on the army—probably due to the influence of my grandfather, who was a colonel in World War II. OSS. And I left because of a major rift between myself and a superior."

Melanie couldn't imagine Mac ever having had a superior, but kept her opinion to herself. He didn't need any more praise from her. He also didn't seem to want to continue with this review of his past.

"All right, Mac," she said, sighing. "If you'd rather not tell me any more of your past, that's fine, but I still haven't the foggiest idea about the present. What's going on now?"

"About six months ago, military intelligence discovered that the programming of one of their satellite computers had been tampered with. After investigating it, the brass knew where it had happened, but not who had done it."

Melanie's eyes widened. "WilCom?" When he nodded, she asked, "But how? Who? Not Frank Wilson. He's too honest."

Mac seemed perturbed. "No, it wasn't Frank. In fact, he has been instrumental in our investigation. It was through him that this whole operation was set up."

"So, who is it? And for that matter, what are they doing?"

"I don't know who, but I have my suspects. And the what is something I had just discovered the afternoon of the day we met. Whoever it is, is using a United States government satellite computer to steal information."

This was not making sense to Melanie. "Well, you must know what they were stealing, or why would you know anybody was doing anything?"

His laugh was a bit forced. "You're pretty sharp, you know that?"

"Yeah, I know. So?"

"So." He sighed. "One of the specialists on the satellite project found an unauthorized code in the communications program."

"Oh," Melanie murmured. "Someone was where they weren't supposed to be?"

"Right."

"How did they do it, hacking?" She had heard about the amazing things people—especially teenagers—were able to do with computers.

"No, well, at least not totally." Mac sighed. "There was hacking done, but whoever did it knew what they were looking for and knew how to get into the system."

Melanie folded her legs beneath her on the seat. "Mac, do you know who is responsible for this? It wasn't those men who kidnapped you?"

He shook his head. "No, they were only goons. Whoever is behind this hired them."

"Why did they go after you? How did they know you had anything to do with the investigation?"

He shrugged. "I don't know that they did. What they did find out was that I hid something, and now they can't find it."

"What?"

"I didn't break the code to find the file in question until that afternoon we met. When I found out what it was, I tried to copy the file and then destroy it, but I didn't have time to break those codes. Every file can be locked under a separate code. So, I hid the entire file under my own code. I couldn't copy it because they were already tracing me, but I slowed them down. I still don't know where they were sending the information. I had just informed the project headquarters of my findings when I was taken on a scenic tour of the Oregon coastline."

Melanie shuddered in remembrance of the sight of Mac falling unconscious to the ground and the sight of the gun. Then she realized that Mac was squeezing her hand.

"That's basically all I know, Melanie. They were hoping to get me to give them the code. It's only a matter of time until they break my code. That's why I have to get back to Bayview. I have to try to get it before they do and to find out who is behind it all. I'm sorry you were dragged into it, but if you won't go into protective custody, then I want to keep an eye on you myself."

Melanie tensed, and she tried not to grip his hand too tightly. How was she going to survive being around him constantly for however long it took for Kyle and Mac to solve their case? She tried to focus on details instead of the whole picture. "Well, won't they still be looking for you?"

He shrugged noncommittally, and Melanie knew he meant yes, but that he was going anyway. He wasn't someone who would stay away because he was in danger. The only reason he had left in the first place was because he had had amnesia.

"Well, I hope you have the sense to be careful."

Mac smiled at her and lifted her fingers to his lips. "Why? Would you miss me if—"

Melanie jerked her hand away. "Don't even joke about that, Mac. It is not funny in the least."

"Hey, I'm sorry." He sounded contrite. "Don't worry. Nothing is going to happen to me."

His confidence did little to assuage Melanie's fear. She still had a memory of a man on an overlook with a gun to Mac's head.

Chapter Eight

As they sped silently down the highway, Melanie waged a silent war with herself. Her head and her heart were fighting over how to handle the mess she was in. She had never had conflicts before. But, then, she'd never met anyone like Mac. Whereas her head had always ruled in the past, her heart refused to budge now. Her love for him was stronger than anything else. In one week, MacAuley Chandler had undermined a lifetime of easygoing noncommitment.

"It doesn't matter, you know."

His voice startled her. She turned away from the window and considered the stubborn set of his jaw.

"What do you mean?"

Mac glanced at her briefly, his eyes narrowed and deliberative. "It doesn't matter what you think of to try to wiggle out of our relationship. It won't work. You belong to me now, and that is the way it's going to stay."

Melanie's eyes were round as she stared at him, then she snapped in anger, "I do not belong to you, Mr. Chandler. I am my own person. And I happen to think that one of us should begin to exercise a little common sense here. God knows it's about time.''

''You can use all the common sense you want, but it won't change the way I feel about you, and it won't change the way you feel about me.''

Melanie fell silent for a minute, struggling to maintain her composure. She wanted so much to believe him, to trust that he was right, but she couldn't deny their unusual circumstances.

''Look, Mac, we have both just come off a very strange and emotionally taxing few days. I'm not saying that what we felt wasn't real, but I am genuinely concerned that away from the cabin and the mountains and all, we both might have serious doubts, and I don't think we should be afraid to express those feelings.''

She wasn't sure he would buy it. She knew that she would never love anyone but MacAuley Chandler, but she didn't want him to feel trapped by things he had said and done while he had had amnesia.

''You have got to stop reading those magazines, sweetheart.''

His flip reply caught her off guard, and before she could open her mouth to protest, he held out a placating hand. ''Before you get all indignant, let me just say that I agree. Sort of.''

''Sort of?''

''I will not concede your point that I was some sort of feeble-minded fool for the last few—''

''I never said any such—''

''Whatever,'' he said, and she let him continue. ''However, I do think that we need time to sort things out.''

She felt a tightness in her heart and fought the urge to cry.

"What I propose," he was saying, "is that we just continue to see each other as we would have if none of this memory stuff had happened."

Melanie gazed at him in confusion. "But we weren't seeing each other."

"Sure we were. Didn't we have a date for dinner last Friday?"

She smiled. "Well, yes, but—"

"All right. Things were just sort of speeded up over the weekend. Why don't we just pick up where we left off and see what happens?"

The casual tone of his voice caused Melanie to raise an eyebrow. She regarded his deceptively calm face and nodded.

"Why do I get the feeling that I don't have a say in the matter anymore?"

"You have lots of say," he answered smoothly. "You can say when, where, how..."

"But can I say no?"

His eyes met hers swiftly. "I don't know. Can you? I know I can't."

Melanie tore her eyes from his and tried to steady her breathing. Why did he always have to be right? Especially about her reaction to him. He knew she would never be able to say no to his sexy eyes and his sensuous mouth. So she gave up, and stared out the window, noting absently that they were on the outskirts of Lansport.

Mac turned off the highway and onto the road that led to Nancy's house. Melanie automatically turned and scanned the area, searching for the dark sedan she knew would haunt her dreams forever.

"I wish you wouldn't do that."

Mac's quiet statement broke the silent tension in the car and startled Melanie. She turned to look at him. He was cautiously eyeing the area himself, but not quite in such an agitated manner.

"Well, I am sorry," she whispered. "You may be confident, but I am more than a little worried about being seen by those men."

"Why are you whispering?" he whispered to her. "They aren't in the car with us."

"Don't you dare laugh at me, Wendell Chandler. If you had the sense God gave a goat, you would be scared, too."

"Sorry," he whispered again. "And don't call me Wendell. My name is Mac."

"Your name is going to be mud if you keep making fun of me."

"Try not to worry. If what Kyle told me is true, then we really shouldn't have to worry...yet."

Melanie didn't like his phrasing.

"Yet? What is that supposed to do? Set my mind at ease?"

Mac stopped at a stop sign.

"You know, sometimes you can be really hyper."

"Well, sorry. But having my life threatened does tend to make me a little crazy. You can go."

"Huh?"

"There's no traffic. You can go."

He shook his head and chuckled and then continued toward Nancy's house.

The street showed no sign of the dark sedan, and Mac pulled into the driveway. A silver Mustang convertible sat in front of the garage, and Mac parked behind it. Melanie jumped out and ran to the porch. She pushed the door open and went in without knocking.

Nancy and Kyle were in the kitchen, cooking. Melanie smiled tentatively when they looked up at her.

"We're here," she offered lamely. Mac entered just behind her then and the four of them stood and stared at each other.

Nancy broke the silence, calmly stating the obvious. "Kyle and I thought you might be hungry, so we're heating up some leftovers."

Melanie shrugged. She and Mac had stopped at a roadside diner for dinner, but that had been hours ago. "I guess—"

"Thanks," Mac answered smoothly. "We appreciate it."

They all sat down and picked at the food, except for Kyle, who seemed to enjoy himself immensely. Mac scowled at his brother constantly, and Nancy and Melanie made small talk.

After dinner, Nancy brought up something Melanie hadn't even thought about.

"Mac," she said, leaning in the doorway between the kitchen and living room, "since you got your memory back, do you remember the two men who attacked you? The police said they couldn't do anything unless you could give descriptions."

Mac shrugged, glancing at Kyle, who sat in the other armchair, next to his. "They weren't very distinctive." Kyle understood, but nodded for him to continue. "I could give general descriptions, but it would be hard to pick those guys out of a lineup."

Melanie nodded, remembering that she had noted how average looking the men were. Then she frowned.

"I thought the same thing when I saw them. I remember trying to memorize their features for a police sketch, but I couldn't pick out one distinctive feature."

Nancy laughed. "Too bad you didn't have your camera ready. You could have snapped them in the act."

"But I did," Melanie countered.

Kyle and Mac seemed to lean forward as one. Melanie instinctively sank back into the cushions of the sofa. "What are you talking about? What camera?'' Kyle's words were casual, but Melanie caught the intensity in his voice.

Blinking in confusion for a moment, Melanie frowned, wondering how she had lost the thread of the conversation. ''I, uh, was taking some pictures of the old Strand Theater on the square...it's boarded up now...I'm doing a story on it. Anyway,'' she hurried on when Mac quirked a dark eyebrow at her, ''I saw you at the telephone booth, and I snapped a few pictures of you. As it happened, Heckel and Jeckel decided to kidnap you at that moment. Is this important? Could those pictures be of any use? I only got one of the two guys.''

''Use?'' Kyle blurted. ''Are you kidding? They could help put that guy in a position to bargain with the attorney general's office for a confession in exchange for a lighter sentence.''

Melanie retrieved her camera bag from the closet and unzipped it. After examining several rolls of film, she handed one to Kyle.

Mac seemed to be considering the information. ''How did you know I was using the pay phone?''

His question caught her off guard. Should she tell him she had been watching him? She scratched her head and looked up at him.

''Well, Wendell, I cannot tell a lie. I noticed you leaving the phone booth as I was changing the lenses on my camera. After all, that black car of yours is a wee bit conspicuous around Bayview.''

''Oh, yeah.'' His comment was a bit sheepish. Then he sobered.

''About my car...''

She groaned as Kyle laughed. ''No more about the car. It's in the backyard.''

Mac looked indignant. ''I was just...I happened to have something very important in that car.''

Melanie caught Nancy's eyes and picked up her purse. After rifling through it for a few seconds, she pulled out the spiral notebook. "This, maybe?"

Mac's eyebrows shot up as he took it from her. "Yes. It has computations for the code—never mind. I'm just glad it's safe."

His eyes were warm, and Melanie smiled back at him. Then she looked away and wondered what she had been planning on doing before thoughts of him chased away all the others.

"I have to call Liane," she said after a minute. "I have to make sure she's all right."

She dialed the familiar number, her fingers gripping the receiver as she thought about the possibility of whoever was behind this knowing that Liane was her sister. After four rings, Liane's husband answered the phone with a cheery hello.

"Chuck? This is Melanie."

"Hi, Mel! How was the weekend in the mountains?"

If you only knew, Chuck. "Uh, it was fine. How is everything there?"

"Fine, like always. You want to talk to Liane?"

Melanie felt her fear leave her body, taking most of her strength with it.

"No, Chuck, that's all right. I was just calling to let her know I was back in town and that I'll be over one day soon to tell her all about it."

Chuck seemed to sense her mood and said, "Sure, Melanie, anytime. You know that. Say, are you all right?"

Melanie managed a weak smile. "Yes, I'm fine, Chuck. Tell Liane I said hello."

"Sure thing. Bye."

"Bye."

"Don't worry," Mac said, pulling the receiver from her fingers and hanging it up. "Everything will be all right."

Melanie was comforted by his words, but she couldn't help but wonder who was going to keep him from getting hurt while he was watching out for her.

The next morning Melanie awoke slowly, with a sense of love and security that emanated from the warm body of Mac, lying next to her on the sofa, his face buried in a cushion, his right arm around her waist. They had fallen asleep together, not wanting to leave each other, needing to be close.

She lay there, not moving for fear of disturbing him, letting herself regain consciousness without struggle. She contemplated their brief but event-filled relationship. How was it possible, she mused, that just two weeks ago she had not even been aware of the existence of Wendell MacAuley Chandler? She knew with absolute certainty that if he were to walk out of her life, she would be devastated.

She wasn't so trite as to think she would die without him; she knew she would live, but her life would have a huge void that only Mac could fill. It was a terrifying thing to know that one person could hold such complete control over her happiness.

She turned her head and looked at his relaxed features. He was so beautiful. Her heart overflowed with love for him, respect for his mind and opinions and a tender desire to make him happy. She knew she would do anything for him, anything he asked. She just prayed that when the excitement of this misadventure had calmed, he would not simply walk out of her life with a quick wave and no forwarding address.

As she watched him, he opened his eyes and smiled at her. His arm tightened around her waist, and he leaned over to kiss her cheek.

"Good morning."

His voice was husky with sleep. Melanie turned and threaded her fingers through his dark hair and whispered, "Good morning."

They talked quietly until they heard Kyle moving around in the guest room, then they rose and started their day.

After they had showered and dressed, the four sat down over doughnuts, orange juice and coffee and discussed their plans. Mac revealed more of the overall picture to Melanie when Kyle admitted that he had told Nancy what they were doing.

At Mac's skeptical expression, Kyle looked chagrined. "She could get information out of a rock. Besides, she already knew..."

Mac waved at him to shut up. "Yeah, yeah. Same song, second verse."

Melanie and Nancy refused to comment. Mac continued his explanation. "I used to be a computer specialist in army intelligence," he began.

"Just before I was to reenlist again, I discovered that there were some secret documents in a computer file I was running a routine check on. When I asked about them, I got a runaround and some drivel about top-secret classification."

Melanie nibbled on a doughnut and asked, "Isn't that possible? I mean, couldn't it have been something that you weren't cleared for?"

Mac shook his head. "No, I thought of that, too, but then I got to thinking about the fact that the people who were telling me that didn't have any higher clearance than I did. And mine is pretty high. No. If they had been in on something that big, so would I. I knew they were up to something, but I didn't know what. I spent about two months trying to figure what they were doing without them finding out about it."

Melanie nodded, then asked, "Did you?"

"No, they started suspecting me, so I had to cool it. But I knew something was happening. A few weeks later, I initiated the paperwork to resign my commission."

"Why?"

He shrugged and tapped a blunt fingertip on the table. "I realized that my immediate supervisor was up to his eyeballs in whatever was going on, and I didn't want him to know what I knew. I also didn't want the project to be put in any danger. After I got stonewalled one too many times, I knew that it was pretty big and that I wasn't accomplishing much on my own. That's when I revealed my suspicions to the project brass."

Melanie didn't try to hide her confusion. "Didn't the other people you were working with wonder why you suddenly left?"

Mac glanced over at Kyle, then nodded. "Yes, but there wasn't much they could do. I told the others on the project that I was opening my own consulting business. I had planned on doing just that upon retirement anyway. If they suspected anything, they kept it to themselves. Of course, I didn't expect the man I was investigating to confront me about my decision to leave."

Nancy frowned. "Well, what about the project 'brass' you mentioned?"

"General Treanor, the head of the communications bureau for the Western Region. He and I were on a tactical team a few years ago, and I trust him. He agreed with my suspicions and promised to see it through, no matter who ended up being incriminated. The thing is, right after I left, everything came to a halt. All the suspicious entries disappeared. Then, a few months later, they discovered another unauthorized code in another top-secret computer. My former superior was in on both projects. That was when the general called me. He knew about Kyle's connection to the Bureau, so a little undercover operation was set up."

This was beginning to sound a little too unreal for Melanie. "Just exactly how important is this little mission of yours?"

"I think you realize how important it is. I know that Kyle has decided that you both have a need to know what is happening because of how involved and at risk you are. We know you can be trusted, but I think that you should also understand the importance of keeping this quiet. We are in the middle of a national security operation that depends upon our controlling what they know about us."

"Oh, my God," Melanie whispered.

She tried to think of something to say, but her mind was a wasteland. She listened to, but didn't participate in, the conversation as Mac and Kyle mapped out their plans for the next few crucial days. After they finally settled on a mutually satisfying plan of action, there was a long silence.

"Since we don't need to do anything for several hours," Melanie finally said calmly, "what do you say to watching a movie?"

Mac stared at her as if she had lost what little mind she had left. "You want to go to see a movie? We can't go out—it's too risky."

Melanie set her jaw. "It isn't just a movie. I was supposed to review it and haven't yet. I told my editor I would have the review on his desk by tomorrow afternoon. Nancy can go get the video from my desk, and we can watch it right here." Nancy nodded her agreement. "And it would be better than sitting around worrying about what might happen."

She expected Mac to put up an argument, but instead, he merely stared at her for a full minute, then nodded. "Maybe you're right."

Nancy and Kyle left to go to the newspaper offices to get the tape. Mac and Melanie sat in the living room staring at each other.

"Are you angry with me?" she finally asked. "Because if you are, just tell me and get it over with. I can't stand silence."

Mac covered her hand with his own. "No, I'm not angry. I'm just worried. And concerned about you."

Melanie felt her eyes threaten to mist over at his statement. "Don't worry about me, Wendell, it'll take more than a national security threat to get rid of me."

He laughed and shook his fist at her. "Mac. My name is Mac."

She smiled smugly at him.

Kyle and Nancy returned with the video and lunch in bags from a local take-out restaurant. They all tried to keep a normal conversation going, purposely ignoring why they were all there. After lunch Nancy put the videocassette in her machine, and they all tried to pay attention.

The film was a pleasant comedy. The characters were romantic adventurers, but with all that had been going on in Melanie's life, the movie seemed tepid. Not that it was a bad film. Neither was it particularly good. Although nothing of any real value, it served its purpose in temporarily taking Melanie's mind off of her present predicament. She took notes on various aspects of the film—acting, directing, writing, scenic design. She forced herself to concentrate on her reviewing instead of on Mac, sitting next to her, or on what awaited them. When the last of the movie's credits had rolled past, Melanie jotted a few last-minute notes and then began writing her review out in longhand.

Nancy walked over to the video player and pressed the button to rewind the tape. Then they all sat down to attempt normal conversation. It wasn't possible. Their minds were all centered on one thing and nothing else.

"The equipment van will be arriving here tomorrow from Salem," Kyle said. "We had to put things on hold for a while until Wendell here regained his senses."

Mac growled a warning to his little brother not to use his first name, then pulled out the spiral notebook and began going over his calculations. Kyle opened his briefcase and reviewed some notes, stopping every few minutes to make telephone calls. Taking their cue, Nancy turned on some quiet music and puttered about, straightening her living room and kitchen.

The strained atmosphere existed until early evening. Nancy and Melanie were grateful for the diversion of fixing dinner, and they went overboard, making a huge lasagna and salad, with a chocolate cake for dessert.

Dinner was a respite from the anxieties of the day, but after the dishes had been done and everyone returned to the living room, the foursome was again at a loss.

Tossing his notebook onto the coffee table, Mac sighed in frustration. "I'm so close. I just need a computer." When Kyle turned to him, Mac waved him off. "I know, the van will be here tomorrow. I just don't want to wait. The thought that they're working on my code makes me nervous. They could find that file anytime." Grinning at Nancy, he asked, "I don't suppose you have a personal computer with a modem and—no, I suppose not."

Nancy shrugged apologetically. "Sorry. Machines and I are mutually suspicious of each other. Melanie's the one who works on a computer."

Kyle and Mac looked at each other, and Melanie missed the smile they shared after Kyle nodded. Still engrossed in her review, she didn't notice Nancy's eyes sparkle with amusement when she understood what they were about. It was the silence that finally brought up Melanie's auburn head. She frowned when she saw the three of them staring at her.

"What?" she asked. Kyle laughed. "It might work. I didn't scrutinize the system, but I think it was pretty sophisticated, for a small-town paper."

"What are you talking about?"

Mac leaned forward, his black eyes glinting mischievously. "What kind of computer system does the newspaper office have?"

Finally catching on to the direction he was headed in, Melanie set her review aside and sat up straighter. "I don't know all its capabilities. All I know is that I write my stories at a terminal, punch a key and it gets stored."

"Is the system linked to other newspapers—other computers?" Mac asked.

"Sure. A few years ago the *Herald* was bought by a newspaper chain. We're linked with other small papers along the coast. Why?"

Kyle laughed. "Do you think it might work?"

"It's worth a try," Mac replied. "Is there anyone at the paper at night, Melanie?"

"No," she answered. "It's only a weekly paper. Oh, the custodian might be there. He works until midnight, I think."

Rising and rubbing his hands, Mac said, "Well, then, let's go. Do you have the keys to the building?"

Melanie gazed at his outstretched hand and smiled. "Sorry. The only people who have the keys are the publisher, the editor, the editor's secretary and the aforementioned custodian. Most of the reporters only work a few days a week, so there isn't a need for all of us to have keys."

At Mac's look of obvious disappointment, she raised her eyebrows conspiratorially. "Of course, I do know of a way to get in. It isn't exactly legal, but, then again, I doubt that Mr. Striker would have me arrested. He likes me."

"Who is Striker?" Mac growled.

Melanie was a little surprised by his tone of voice. "The publisher," she answered, wondering even more when Mac smiled easily and nodded.

"So, how do I get in?"

Melanie rose and looked from Mac's expectant face to Kyle's curious one. "Alone? You don't. But I'll show it to you."

There ensued a heated discussion where Mac refused to let her come, Kyle tried to coax her cooperation, and Nancy just shook her head in amusement. Melanie finally just picked up her review, folded it and stuck it in her back pocket. She picked up Nancy's keys and dangled them in front of Mac.

"Come on. I'm going. Accept it." Turning to Kyle, she asked, "Are you and Nancy coming, too?"

Kyle glanced over at Nancy, who stood and waited. "Sure. Why not? We'll be lookouts or getaway drivers or whatever."

Melanie was perceptive enough to realize that Kyle's joking had a thread of seriousness about it. He didn't seem to expect any trouble, but he was going to be prepared for it, just in case.

Mac rubbed his neck and picked up his spiral notebook. "Great. Why don't we just have a parade or make an announcement?"

Pushing him toward the door, Melanie decided he was really enjoying all of this. "Quit your grousing, Wendell. Accept the fact that I won't be left out."

She continued pushing him toward the car. He finally stopped, and Melanie knew that no amount of pushing on her part would budge him unless he wanted to be budged. Turning, he frowned down at her.

"If you don't stop calling me Wendell..." His threat trailed off as Melanie began to laugh.

"What are you going to do, Wendell?"

He continued to gaze down into her grinning face, illuminated by the front porch light, and then, without warning, he kissed her. Melanie was immediately lost in the sensations created by his lips and tongue. He held her lightly but firmly. She knew that she could have pulled away if she had wanted to. But she didn't.

"What is this? If you were just trying to get away to neck, why did you invite us along?"

Kyle's amused voice cut through Melanie's jumbled thoughts, but Mac took his time pulling away from her. Then he was pushing her toward the car. She allowed him to seat her in the back seat, then he followed her. Kyle and Nancy got into the front seat.

"If that's your idea of carrying out a threat, Wendell," Melanie murmured, "I wonder what you would do if I printed your name in the newspaper?"

His low chuckle sent tingles along the surface of her skin. "Want to find out?"

"I don't know," she mused. "It might be...dangerous."

"Dangerous?" He considered her words. "No, not dangerous. At least not in the physical sense."

"That's what I was afraid of."

Thrity-five minutes later they were getting out of the car, across from the alley that would lead to the newspaper building. Kyle didn't think that there was any danger of their being spotted, but taking precautions couldn't hurt, either.

It was agreed that Kyle and Nancy would cruise the area until they saw a signal from Mac—a flicker of a lighter—that he had either accomplished his goal with the computer or that it wasn't going to work. As the car drove away, Mac leaned over and started to say something. Melanie placed her hand over his mouth and shook her head.

"Forget the last-minute plea for me to stay out of it, Wendell. Don't forget, I'm the one who knows how to get into the building quietly and quickly."

She removed her hand, and he kissed her warmly. She sighed and began to relax against him. He then abruptly pushed her away from him and laughed soundlessly.

"Later," he promised, and they made their way into the alley.

They walked quietly and swiftly down the alley and, after checking the area, proceeded to the next alley up a block. Melanie let Mac lead the way, watching his firmly muscled body with confidence, knowing that he could be trusted with her life. But, when they reached the building in which the newspaper was housed, Melanie pulled at his sweater and demanded the lead. After a brief silent argument, in which there were many fierce stares and much hand waving, Melanie stepped in front of Mac and decided that if he wanted to stand there, he could. Or he could follow her. He followed.

Melanie moved quickly, her body bent slightly, her feet, shod in tennis shoes borrowed from Nancy, moving silently on the pavement of the walk used by the employees and the delivery people.

When she reached a side door, she paused. Mac was right behind her, giving her a sense of security and confidence. She pointed at the window above them, and he nodded. The wide, industrial window was about seven feet above the ground. On the other side were the presses of the newsroom.

Mac took Melanie's hands and leaned to one side, creating a step out of his thigh. She stepped on it and was then settled on his shoulders. She leaned forward and pushed at the right side of the window. It resisted only slightly and then swung inward with a squeak Melanie knew must have been heard for miles. She looked down at Mac. He just looked up at her, his expression resigned.

With a helpful boost from Mac she climbed through the open window, swung her legs over the sill, then lowered herself to the other side, almost knocking over a water cooler in the process. She let herself drop to the floor after making certain there was nothing below her. Then she ran to the door and unlocked it for Mac. When he didn't immediately enter the building, she felt a wave of panic engulf her as a dozen horrific scenarios flashed through her mind, not the least of which was a repeat—complete with ending—of the attempt on Mac's life at the overlook.

Just as she started to run through the door to search for him, he backed into the building, his attention on the possible points of entry from the street. Melanie ran full force into his broad back and was knocked off balance, falling back on her rear on the floor of the press room. Mac whirled around, and looked amused at the sight of Melanie sitting on the floor.

"What is so funny, Wendell?" she asked, and then the relief of seeing him safe overwhelmed her. She lay back on the floor with her arms crossed over her chest, and she whispered her own epitaph in a solemn voice. "She expired due to a cardiac arrest brought on by shock."

Mac chuckled softly and bent to help her to her feet. "Scared to death, huh?"

Melanie brushed off her pants and tried to appear calm, although she was sure that Mac could see her heart beating through her sweater, even in the near darkness. "I wouldn't think that you would be so smug, since it would have been you who would have been responsible for my death."

"I'm sorry if I scared you, Melanie, but I had to check for possible intruders."

"We are the intruders, Mac. I'm just glad I went to the bathroom before we left."

He laughed again and then followed her out of the room. They spotted the custodian—asleep in his small office. Determined not to wake him, they climbed the stairs to the third-floor offices. The first thing they both did was to go over to the windows and surreptitiously scan the street. A sense of security settled over her as Melanie saw Nancy and Kyle driving by, inconspicuous among the few other vehicles driven mainly by teenagers cruising in search of other teenagers.

Mac pulled Melanie away from the window. "They don't know we're here, yet. But they might have a trace on the computer modem. We won't have much time once I access the file," he said softly. "Come on. Where is the terminal with the modem?"

Melanie showed him the terminal on the desk of a co-worker, and he settled behind it, expertly operating the machine, which cast an eerie green glow around him.

"It will only take me a few minutes to access the computer files, but then I'll need a floppy disk to copy them on, and—" He looked around quickly, searching through the darkness. "Does this thing have a printer?"

Melanie pointed to an adjacent table where an expensive printer sat. Mac nodded. "Good. It's a quiet one. Could you find some computer paper and a blank floppy disk?"

Melanie nodded and went looking through the unlocked drawers of the nearby desks. She found the computer paper easily enough, and, after loading it, went in search of a floppy disk. Mac was still engrossed in punching the keys of the computer.

She rifled the drawers of the food editor, knowing that she kept recipes on floppy disks for reference. Finding a box of disks and not knowing if any were blank, Melanie took one that had no label and rationalized that if Darlene didn't want them erased, she should label them. She returned to Mac just as he was finishing his search for the file. She handed him the disk, and he inserted it into the computer's disk drive and punched a few more keys.

There was a brief pause and then a file popped onto the screen. Mac grunted and punched more keys after looking at his spiral notebook. Melanie was holding her breath. She knew that it was more than likely that someone was trying to trace them. Mac was still furiously punching the keys. Then he stabbed the air with his fist.

"Yeah!" he said softly. Melanie assumed he had finally broken one of the codes. He looked at his watch and swore. There were a lot of technical terms that Melanie didn't understand on the screen, and she wasn't about to ask Mac for a lesson in computer language now. Just as she was about to walk away and leave Mac to his copying, she noticed some new symbols appearing on the screen. These were different. They were drawings—technical blueprints of what appeared to be an airplane. Or more precisely, a fighter jet.

She must have reacted by squeezing Mac's shoulder, because he had raised his hands and placed them on hers. They both understood the seriousness of what they were doing. Melanie didn't know what the file was about—other than the fact that it was a matter of national security. Whatever it was, Mac was sufficiently worried about it to go to all these lengths to thwart the men in the dark sedan and the people who had hired them.

When the file had been copied, Mac removed the disk from the drive and placed it into the drive of a nearby computer. He tested the disk to make sure the file had been copied and then he turned back to the computer in front of him and entered new commands. Melanie was desperately curious, but knew that she shouldn't interrupt him. She waited until he was done typing. The file disappeared. She was about to ask about his motives when she noticed that on the screen where the text had been, Mac was inputting something of his own. It was a message. It was brief but to the point.

Let's play a game. It's called hide-and-seek.

Melanie suddenly knew what it meant. As Mac snapped off the computer, she whispered, "You hid it again, didn't you?"

He nodded and pocketed the floppy disk. "I did. I wanted to erase it, but I don't have the time to figure out how to unlock it. It took too long to jump the copy block. But it should take them quite a while to find it. Hopefully, enough time to get the feds here to arrest them."

Melanie looked at the printer. Mac was punching the keys of the computer hooked up to the printer. Within minutes the file had been printed. Mac tore the paper off and folded it, placing it in his back pocket. He put the floppy disk in a plastic sheath and stuck it in the back of his waistband. He turned off the computer and the printer and then turned to Melanie.

"We may need a red herring, so to speak. Can you get me a disk with something—anything—on it?"

Melanie was gone and back in thirty seconds with one of Darlene's recipe files. Mac put it with the real disk. Melanie left for a minute to put her review on her editor's desk, with a note explaining nothing and apologizing for the review not being typed.

She and Mac made their way back down to the press room, retracing their steps to arrive at the back door. Mac opened the door a crack and checked the area. He waited for what seemed like hours to Melanie, even though she knew it was really only a few minutes. He then pulled a lighter from his pocket and held it above his head, flicking it on and letting the flame burn for a few seconds before snapping it off.

"Did you see them?" she whispered.

He nodded, and together they waited another minute before Mac again opened the door and peered outside. By this time, Kyle, having seen the signal, would be back where they had parted, across from the alley.

Melanie, her hand on Mac's back, waited for him to ease out the door. When he did, she followed, stopping to make sure the door had locked behind them. Then they made their way back to the car, where Kyle immediately asked if Mac had been successful.

Sliding into the back seat next to Melanie, Mac slapped the bucket seat where Kyle sat. "'Successful' isn't the word, brother. Wait until you see what I've got. This is great."

As Kyle drove, he kept looking into the rearview mirror, squinting to make out Mac's expressions in the dark. "So...what? Are you just going to drop that bombshell and then shut up?"

"You know what it is, since I found it last week, but it still has got to be seen to be fully appreciated. Words don't do it justice."

When they entered the house, Mac waited until everyone was seated, then he pulled out the computer printout and the disk and dropped them on the coffee table. Then he sank onto the sofa next to Melanie.

Kyle reached eagerly for the paper, unfolding it with an expression on his face very like a small child's on Christmas. His intelligent eyes scanned the information, and he whistled softly when he saw what it was. Rising, he headed for the telephone.

"You weren't kidding, Mac. This is a beaut. General Treanor is going to be very interested in this. Not to mention a few people I work for."

Nancy yawned, murmured something about it being a good idea for all of them to get some sleep and went into her bedroom. Kyle, having informed his superiors of the latest development, likewise turned in.

Melanie gazed at Mac with a tired intensity she was unaware of. He looked up at her, and she saw that same intensity reflected in his eyes.

She didn't look away in embarrassment at being caught staring at him. She merely continued to stare, remaining silent. Mac returned her scrutiny. After an indeterminable amount of time, Melanie slowly inched closer to him. At first he didn't touch her or say anything. He just looked at her. Then she snuggled into his side, and he put his arms around her. She laid her head on his chest, listening to his heartbeat, strong and steady. He rested his chin on the top of her auburn head, and they stayed that way until Melanie fell asleep in his arms.

Chapter Nine

They awoke in the morning to a flurry of activity. The phone began ringing at 6:00 a.m. and didn't seem to rest after that. Either Kyle was calling his associates or they were calling him. Mac spoke with military personnel familiar with the case, then Liane called to make sure Melanie was all right.

Nancy and Melanie watched the proceedings with apprehension and not a little awe. They made breakfast and then lunch, talking quietly and leaving the Chandler brothers to work. They caught enough snatches of conversation to know generally what was going on, but Melanie had a feeling that there were more secrets, and she wasn't sure she wanted to know what they were.

Kyle left to rendezvous with his associates, who were in a van setting up their equipment. Nancy had threatened to follow him when he meant to leave her at home, but he relented when she suggested that she would be safer with him than alone.

Later, Mac talked with his brother on the telephone, and although she wasn't sure, Melanie thought that they had set up the final phase of their operation.

Just before darkness fell, she saw Mac standing before the picture window, staring into the fading sunset. He looked tense but not worried, and Melanie suddenly felt reassured. She had complete confidence in this man and trusted him implicitly. She loved him. She knew that he at least cared for her. Finding out just how deep his feelings were for her was what mattered. Everything else seemed unimportant to her. And she would find out. She smiled just as he looked over at her.

"What?"

Melanie shook her head. "Nothing in particular. I just have a feeling that everything is going to be all right. Better than all right."

He smiled. "Yes, well, let's take that as an omen of good luck."

Melanie raised an eyebrow. "Do you think we'll need it?"

"Couldn't hurt."

She frowned. Maybe he was worried and just hiding it. He was usually the one who was cheerful and minimized the danger. "Are you really worried, Mac?"

He shrugged. "Not for myself. Kyle is very good at what he does. I trust him with my life, and what's more important is that I trust him with your life. But even he isn't perfect."

Melanie smiled softly. He was worried about her. "I'll be all right, Mac. I promise to do whatever you say, but don't ask me not to come with you."

He sighed in resignation.

"Okay," she said, smiling. "What did Kyle say when he called?"

Mac turned to face her and rested his hands on the back of an armchair. "He said that they took the bait, but that doesn't mean they believe our cover story... but black-mailing them for the disk is logical. It really would be at a premium in certain markets. Besides, it's necessary. The only evidence the FBI has so far is circumstantial. They're hoping that this operation will get some hard evidence—something that can stand up in court. And they want to get everyone involved. I told you about the officer I worked with... well, we don't have any conclusive evidence against him or any information about who he's working with.''

"Except that they work at WilCom?"

Mac sighed. "Yes. But even that isn't concrete. It's possible that whoever was at WilCom isn't there anymore. Three people with computer access have quit or been fired within the last six months. They, plus all current employees, have to be considered. That's why we're hoping to get what we need tonight. Now that whoever it is has agreed to a meeting, maybe they'll say something incriminating on tape.''

"Does Kyle think that they suspect us of trying to catch them?''

"To a degree, but mainly because they're going to be suspicious of anyone outside their own circle. Especially after what we've done to mess up their plans. That's why we won't find out the location of the meeting until the last minute. That makes it impossible for Kyle to go in and wire the place and secure it." He paused, his expression grim. "They're not as smart as they think they are, and that's in our favor. Kyle has been working with a special team for several weeks on this, and they have everything under control. Every angle has been explored and all the avenues accounted for.

"The meeting with them was set up through the computer, since that was the only way we had of reaching them. Kyle was able to contact them using a portable computer in his van. I think they were expecting us to contact them that way. Kyle is waiting now for them to tell us where the meeting is supposed to take place.''

Melanie felt herself relax a little. Mac wasn't a person who would take life-threatening situations lightly. If he had confidence in Kyle, then so did she. She smiled and nodded. Mac reached over and squeezed her hand.

''You already know that I would rather you didn't come along for this particular ride, and if you have second thoughts—any at all would be more than welcome to me—you only have to give me the word.....''

He had such a hopeful look on his face that Melanie almost hated to turn down the offer. But she had to, and she knew that he was expecting her to do just that.

''No way. I am in this with you until the resolution, as we say in the movie-reviewing business. I have to make sure you don't get knocked on the head again and forget me.''

Mac laughed. ''No chance, sweetheart.''

Melanie felt warm inside. As she gazed into Mac's dark eyes, she felt confident about everything. Not just about the operation tonight, but about their future. She couldn't be wrong about him. It felt too right.

Kyle called a few minutes later and gave Mac the name of an all-night diner on the highway. Melanie shrugged. What did she know about meetings with traitors? She was familiar with the place. It was a dingy greasy-spoon with a single sign that said EAT.

It was a little after nine when they drove toward Bayview. After about twenty minutes driving north on the coast highway, Melanie whispered, ''The diner is about a half mile farther. Kyle said the drive was just past . . . there.'' As Mac pulled off the road onto a private drive Kyle had directed them to, he whispered, ''You're whispering again.''

Melanie hit him with her fist on the muscle of his upper arm. ''Ow!''

"That's what you get for being violent," he said as she rubbed her knuckles.

"Okay," Mac began, his voice serious, "according to the message, they think we have the file."

"We do have the file."

"Not with us, though. Hopefully, it won't matter. We couldn't risk that information. They think we're willing to sell them the disk."

"Okay," Melanie said, thinking aloud. "So, the real disk is with the proper authorities, and we pretend that this one is the real one."

She opened her purse and extracted a disk of software that had Darlene's recipes on it. She put it back into her purse as Mac nodded.

Melanie wondered at the ridiculous way this sounded. Spies. FBI. Traitors. Killers. Coded floppy disks. It was almost more than her small-town mentality could bear. Things like this just did not happen in Bayview, Oregon. San Francisco, yes. Seattle, yes. But not Bayview. Nothing in the least exciting ever happened in Bayview. That is, nothing ever did until Mac Chandler came to town. And Melanie wouldn't change any of it. She thought it ironic that most of the town didn't know—and probably never would know—about any of the excitement that had taken place right in front of them. She blinked her eyes hard to focus her concentration.

"What happens if the alphabet guys aren't in place?"

Mac frowned in the moonlit car. "Then I have this to equalize the situation."

He pulled a gun out of his pocket—it was the one she had taken from his assailants. She hated guns, but she recognized the need for this particular weapon in this particular situation. Mac was trained to use it and knew what he was doing. That calmed her a bit, although not much.

"Now," Mac continued, "I have to get wired, and then we have to get them to talk about the information on the disk, without being obvious about it. We can't let them know that they are being taped, or the whole thing will blow up in our faces."

"No problem." Melanie laughed, forcing it a bit. "You're dealing with someone who not only has seen every spy movie for the last few years, but who also was required to take beginning acting in college."

"How'd you do?"

"Lousy. I got a C, but only because the professor felt sorry for me."

"Well, let's hope you've improved with age."

"What?"

"Nothing. Let's go, it's nine-thirty."

Mac got out of the car and helped Melanie out, then leaned over to pick up her purse, which was sitting on the floorboard. He turned to her in surprise.

"What do you have in this thing? Rocks?"

Melanie took her purse and shouldered it. "Don't be silly. It's just my stuff. Since I no longer have a gun, and don't want one, Nancy and I thought that I should have something in case we got in trouble."

When Mac opened her purse, Melanie sighed. "You don't have to look, I'll tell you. It's just some paperweights and a couple of little marble bookends that Nancy has. She thought I could throw them if need be."

Mac chuckled quietly and shook his head, but didn't say anything.

They then began walking toward a van that was sitting just ahead of them on the private drive, concealed from the highway by an overgrowth of trees and shrubbery. Mac gestured to it and leaned over to whisper in Melanie's ear.

"That's Kyle. He's in there with the recording equipment."

Melanie nodded. She wanted to be professional and spy-worthy, but when she felt Mac's warm breath on her ear and his husky voice vibrating against her sensitive skin, her mind was on things other than spies.

He then took Melanie's hand, and they hurried silently to the rear door of the van, which was slightly ajar. They didn't have to knock. The door opened as they reached it.

There was a faint blue light on, and Melanie noticed that the van was really quite large as she stood in it, surrounded by electronic gizmos and computers. Then she saw Nancy sitting in the front seat. Melanie walked forward and leaned over the seat.

"Hey, what are you doing up here?" she whispered.

Nancy grinned. "Where else did you expect me to be?"

Melanie shook her head. "Silly me."

It was then that Melanie realized there was a fierce argument going on in whispers behind her. She turned and found Mac shaking his head and leaning over an equally stubborn Kyle, who was seated at a computer terminal with another agent, shrugging and pointing at something on the shallow counter that the computer sat on. Melanie could see that it was not going to stop soon. She turned toward them and took one step. They all shut up and looked at her.

"What's the matter?" she said softly.

"Mac doesn't want—"

"Forget it, Kyle."

"Mac," Kyle said patiently, "they'll find it on you."

Melanie finally realized what they were talking about. The microphone.

"What's the problem?" Melanie asked, and then saw what was lying on the counter.

It was an underwire bra. Her brain did a doubletake. Yes, that is what is was. She leaned between the brothers, who had stopped talking and were just staring at each other, and picked up the undergarment.

She held it close to the blue light and studied it.

The front clasp was the microphone. The wires were run through the underwire of the bra. She thought it was really quite ingenious.

"Sorry, Mac, but I don't think it's your size."

Her soft voice broke the silence, and Kyle chuckled quietly as Mac continued to fume. The other agent sat silently at the console, clearing his throat and looking at his watch.

Mac started to protest again, but Nancy stood and hustled the men out of the van. Kyle stopped in front of her and tried to look official.

"Uh, this is a technical matter, you know."

Nancy seemed to be considering his argument. "Uh-huh. Why don't you just let us women handle it?"

"You always get the fun jobs."

"Poor baby. Maybe I can find something fun for you to do later."

His voice lowered to a husky rasp. "I'll hold you to that."

A few minutes later, Kyle made a check to make sure the wire was working, and then the two agents were giving last-minute instructions.

The other agent was introduced only as Joe, and he began to briefly and succinctly outline what was going to happen.

"The meeting was set for ten in the diner. We aren't positive they won't try to pull something, but we're ready for anything. We'll all be in constant communication and will be listening at all times. They'll be expecting a wire, but I don't think they'll find this one. You aren't carrying a concealed weapon, are you?"

The question was routine, but Melanie glanced nervously at Mac, who sighed and pulled out the gun, handing it to Kyle.

"Wendell, don't you know that carrying a concealed weapon without a permit is illegal?"

Mac growled something about teaching Kyle a little brotherly respect and then fell silent. Joe cleared his throat and pointed to the reel-to-reel tape recorder on the counter.

"We will be taping everything. We need you to get them to talk about who did what and how it was accomplished. A complete confession would be nice, but we need details. You have to be careful. Let them talk on their own if they will. Supposedly, they think that you two are trying to blackmail them. Criminals understand other criminals."

"Remember," Kyle added, "that even though we want the evidence, we won't be too far away. We are also confident that neither of you will do anything...rash to jeopardize either yourselves or the operation."

Mac and Melanie looked at each other, then she shrugged. "Don't look at me, I only brought a few paperweights and two bookends. You brought the equalizer." Mac merely closed his eyes.

"We'll leave first and take the van to the diner. Nancy and I will go in first—just a charming couple on a charming vacation," Kyle elaborated. "Joe stays in the van and keeps in touch with me—via this radio." He held up what looked like a hearing aid. "There are three other agents inside with similar devices and microphones. After we get inside, you two pull into the parking lot and come in. Sit near the window. After that, we wait and watch."

Mac nodded, then ushered Melanie out of the van and into Nancy's car. They waited until the van passed them, then watched the illuminated digital clock in the car. When five of the longest minutes in history had elapsed, they followed.

Pulling into the parking lot of the diner, Mac purposely avoided parking next to the van. "This is it," he said softly. "Your last chance to bail out. And I really wish you would."

"You're so sweet when you're being protective, Wendell."

She patted his cheek and opened her door. She heard him swear under his breath as he got out of the car, closing his door and hurrying around to join her.

The sound of car tires on the gravel of the parking lot caused them both to automatically glance toward it. Pulling to a stop behind the Mazda was a dark sedan. Melanie stifled a gasp. The two men who had kidnapped Mac were sitting in the front seat, the one on the passenger side holding a gun.

"Get in," the driver ordered softly. Melanie wondered if his words were loud enough to be picked up by the microphone. "Look, Mac," she said, "our ride's here."

Mac looked a bit startled by her words, but agreed with her. "Yes, I wasn't expecting limo—or even Fairmont—service."

As they walked toward the car, Melanie stole a glance at the diner. She could see Kyle and Nancy sitting at a table near the front windows. Kyle was speaking, and Melanie doubted it was to Nancy.

When Mac and Melanie reached the car, the man on the passenger side got out and stopped them. He looked around the area briefly. "Nice to see you again." Melanie squeezed Mac's arm in a death grip as she looked at the man who had almost killed him a week ago. Then Mac was rapidly frisked and shoved into the back seat.

Melanie stood frozen as the man's hands started to roughly run over her body. She gritted her teeth to stop them from chattering out of fear. "They're clean," he declared as he shoved her into the car next to Mac.

Melanie breathed a mental sigh of relief. Kyle had been right about the wire. They would have found it on Mac. Her purse was pulled from her grasp then and rifled through.

"No weaponry. Just a couple of little sculptures of some dead composer and—looky here." He waved the disk at his partner after dropping Melanie's purse over the front seat.

It dropped in her lap and she winced, trying not to groan. The first man got into the car, and they drove off, leaving Kyle and the other agents behind. Melanie thought this might be a good time to worry.

"Where are we going?" she asked.

"Shut up."

After looking at Mac, who shook his head, she fell silent, looking out the window. About thirty seconds went by before she piped up again. "Why didn't you just tell us we were going into town? We could have met you here, you know. I grew up in Bayview, I know all kinds of—"

"Can't you shut her up?" the driver demanded of Mac.

She felt Mac's fingers tighten on hers. "Apparently not," he answered.

The other hood didn't seem as disinclined to talk as the one driving. He turned, keeping his gun on them and said, "Where you been holed up? You don't know how hard we been lookin' for you two."

"Oh, we have an idea." Mac's voice sounded very cool to Melanie, and she imperceptibly relaxed next to him.

Suddenly they were pulling onto one of the streets that led to the Bayview town square. The driver guided the car through the square and around the back of one street to an alley. The engine was shut off, and the men got out and opened the back doors.

"Come on," the first one said, "there's somebody who wants to see you."

They walked onto the square, one man in front of them and one behind. Melanie had never thought of the Bayview town square as being ominous, but at that moment, she did. Every shadow and crevice seemed sinister. The small-town friendliness was overshadowed by darkness and danger. She didn't like it. She didn't like being afraid of walking in the little town that had been her home for so long. And she was imbued with a renewed desire to rid Bayview of those who had abused her.

They reached the front of the boarded-up movie theater without seeing or hearing anything. The leader stopped just as they reached the doors. The movie theater? Melanie stared at the building.

"Did you know I was writing a story about this theater?" she asked the man behind her, conversationally.

"No," he said, pushing her through the door behind Mac.

The lobby was dark and foreboding. The only source of light came from the streetlamp outside. It filtered in through the cracks between the sheets of plywood that had been nailed over the broken windows. The carpeting was threadbare, the paint had peeled off the walls, but there were still posters proclaiming movies from ten years before hanging on either side of the swinging double doors that led into the main auditorium.

No one was in the lobby or in the office, which was next to the forlorn candy counter, empty of candy or popcorn. Melanie clung tightly to Mac's hand and looked at the swinging doors. There were small, portholelike windows in the doors. It was dark, but there was a glow of light coming from somewhere above the main floor. Melanie glanced up. The house lights weren't on. The light seemed to be coming from the projection room at the back of the balcony.

Mac was looking up at the light when Melanie glanced at his face. When he looked at her, she glanced toward the staircase at the far end of the lobby.

"After you," the leader said. "There is business to attend to, and we wouldn't want to keep your host waiting."

Mac nodded at the gunman. "Of course not. We all want the 'business' to be taken care of soon."

They approached the carpeted staircase and began to ascend. Melanie was practically hidden behind Mac's body, and she squeezed his arm to reassure herself of his strength.

Feeling like a scared rabbit, Melanie was determined to appear like a confident moll—or whatever extortionists' girlfriends were called these days. As they climbed the stairs, she said, "Say, why are the lights off? This place gives me the creeps."

The man behind her laughed and waved the gun. "I kinda like it dark."

Melanie decided it would be wiser not to continue the conversation and followed Mac up the last few steps and onto the balcony. "I used to like the balcony when I was a kid," Melanie offered. "We used to drop food on people."

Her friendly gunman laughed. "Yeah, I used to do that, too."

The leader turned and glared at Melanie. She smiled weakly and shut up, noticing that the man behind her was being glared at, also.

Then they were being led down the aisle to the front row of the balcony. There, two rows back in the center, was the shadow of a man. The light from the projection booth cast a glow around his head, but not on his face. Melanie felt prickles on her arms. Why did he seem familiar when she hadn't seen his face or heard his voice?

"Welcome, Mr. Chandler. Melanie. How pleased I am that you made it here on time."

The house lights suddenly popped on as the second thug flipped a switch, and when Melanie's eyes adjusted, she stared. It was Frank Wilson's junior vice president in charge of marketing, Arnie Edwards. His bland blond looks had always seemed simpy to Melanie. She hadn't given him the credit to mastermind something of this magnitude. She had always just thought of him as another junior executive at WilCom—one she never thought would rise very far in the corporate structure. Melanie tried to appear impassive and struggled to cover her surprise. She spent about two seconds contemplating whether to speak to him.

"Well, well, Arnie Edwards. I would like to say I'm surprised, but now that I think about it, I'm not. You always have been an outsider. No one I know thinks very much of you."

"Ah, Melanie. Ever able to slice through to the bone with a few words. You never seemed one to mince—"

"Now, now, play nice, children," Mac interjected. "Since you two know one another, this should be easy."

Melanie nodded and spread her lips in what passed for a smile. She gestured grandly with her right hand, while keeping a firm grip on her purse with the left.

"Oh, sure. Although Arnie wanted to know me better than I wanted to know him. How many times was it that you asked me out? Six, seven?"

Arnie laughed, but it wasn't a normal sound. To Melanie's ears, it sounded evil and menacing.

"Yes, well, you were always pretending to be too good for me. But now, it would seem that you are the one who is straying from the straight and narrow. What exactly are you planning to do with all the money you are extorting from me?"

Melanie glanced quickly at Mac. She had almost forgotten their reason for being there. She looked back at Arnie.

"I'm giving it to charity."

"Right." He laughed.

Mac gestured at the briefcase sitting next to Arnie.

"Is that it?"

Arnie patted the briefcase. "Yes. But, of course, I have to see what you brought for me, first."

"Of course," Melanie repeated facetiously.

The man who had taken the disk from Melanie handed it to Arnie. Melanie knew they had to stall to keep him from finding out what was really on the disk.

"You know, Arnie, I never would have thought that something like that—" she gestured to the disk "—would interest someone like you."

"Someone like me? What's that supposed to mean?"

Melanie contained her excitement. Was he going to open up and spill it or cough it up or sing or whatever criminals did when they admitted their sins?

"Oh, just that this whole thing seems a little complicated for you. You never seemed that bright."

Arnie's blond brows drew together in an annoyed scowl. Mac's hand tightened on Melanie's waist. She could feel his concern, but she didn't dare look at him. Then Arnie snorted, and Melanie could feel the tenseness leave Mac's hand. The immediate crisis was over. Melanie just hoped there weren't very many more.

"You always were quick with the put-downs, Melanie. That used to really annoy me. People like you are always so self-righteous and law-abiding. Then you turn out to be just as larcenous and unscrupulous as the rest of us. It would seem as if a few of the deadly sins—namely, greed—have shown up to mar your otherwise lily-white surface."

Melanie shrugged. "Maybe. But whatever my motivations are, they pale in comparison to yours. After all, if we're going to play one-upmanship, I know I'd lose. My pathetic attempt at blackmail is diddly next to your little scheme."

Mac must have decided that he was tired of playing the observer. "Actually, the blackmail was my idea, so Melanie doesn't really get the credit for that."

"Ah, yes, the partner in crime. I knew that she was involved after that day on the overlook, but my surprise was that she would be involved in it at all. As a matter of fact, there were those who doubted your ability to be bought, Mr. Chandler.''

Mac's dark brows rose slightly. "Those?"

Arnie nodded. "A certain major serving in the armed forces of this great country of ours. He was quite annoyed at your snooping around. Of course, I'm sure that if he had known that you just wanted a cut of this rather lucrative pie, he would have welcomed you into the fold."

Mac's voice was hard. "Eastman."

"A patriot among patriots," Arnie sneered. "By the by, he couldn't be here this evening as he had a hot date with a marguerita on a tropical isle."

"Why aren't you with him?" Melanie questioned.

"Oh, well, you see, Eastman got a wee bit scared as things got complicated. He took what he had and ran."

"What he had?" Mac asked.

"Yes," Arnie said, slowly, leaning forward slightly. "He could have gotten a lot more if he hadn't been so afraid of you. He didn't believe you could be bought. He kept saying—right up until yesterday—that you were pulling something and that he didn't trust you."

Melanie's brain was racing. Searching for something to say that would put an end to Arnie's suspicions and get him to open up. Mac must have been doing the same thing.

"He was right not to trust me."

Arnie's pale eyes widened visibly at Mac's words. But they narrowed as Mac continued. "Because I would have cut him out as soon as I could. He's a parasite. He doesn't have the brains to come up with an original idea. He can only operate under explicit directions."

Arnie considered this statement for a moment, then nodded. "True. But, then, that's why he was chosen."

Melanie was almost afraid to ask. "Chosen?"

"Sure, you don't think he came to me?"

Mac sounded surprised. "Aren't you being just a bit presumptuous?"

This remark seemed to rankle Arnie. He stood up to face the two of them. Melanie didn't think it was a smart move, psychologically, for Arnie. Mac was the taller by at least four inches.

"Listen, Chandler, I'm no jerk who doesn't know which end is up. This whole deal was possible only because I made it possible! I was the one who set this operation up in the first place. Eastman was a greedy necessity. He was also dispensable. Greed is a common sin. As you both are well acquainted with it, I'm sure you'll agree."

Melanie stared. She could hardly believe it, but he actually sounded proud of his traitorous activities. Knowing she had to continue the charade, she smiled.

"Wow, Arnie. You know, I bet no one in Bayview ever thought you would do anything but three-to-five for being a Peeping Tom." She laughed as he blushed. "That was what I told him that day, Mac. I found out that he had been watching women undress in the corporate locker room. *That* I expected from you, Arnie, but espionage? I mean, how does someone like you get a job like that? What did you do, send a résumé to Moscow?"

She looked at his reddened face and wondered what she could do to get him to say something incriminating. They had to get more information out of him before the federal agents came rushing in to take Arnie's worthless carcass off to jail. At least she hoped that Kyle and Joe had understood her hints about where they had been taken and were now ready to rescue them.

Arnie's smile was feral. "That's very amusing. Especially since you are now operating a few levels below me on the criminal ladder. I'm sure you'll be disappointed to hear, but I am not under exclusive contract to the Soviets. I pledge allegiance to no one save myself. I supply a product and sell it to the highest bidder.''

He glanced at Mac. "Your Major Eastman and I met several years ago, and he was quite willing to work with me when he realized that he could make a lot of money with very little effort on his part. He scouted for clients, and I obtained the desired information. My affinity for computers was our ticket. No travel, no dark alleys or unsavory atmospheres. Everything could be done through computers. Contacts. Transferrals of money. Information delivered. All I had to do was access a few top-secret computers, which wasn't all that difficult given Eastman's clearances, and the rest was easy."

Mac crossed his arms over his chest. "So, you worked yourself out quite a little deal, huh? Very little danger and a lot of reward."

"That's right. And now that I have the information you stole, I can be on my way to a more opulent life-style. There are, after all, those in this wonderful world who appreciate, and are willing to compensate, enterprising men like myself." He brought a forefinger to his lips.

"And by the way, I have to congratulate you for erasing that file. I thought I had covered all the exits."

Mac let one eyebrow raise. "I didn't erase it. I just hid it again. It's still in the system."

"What?"

"Hide-and-seek, Arnie," Melanie murmured.

"And I doubt that you have the time to look for it," Mac added. "The people you deal with aren't known for their patience."

Arnold didn't seem to appreciate being fooled. He seemed to be turning purple. Then he smiled.

"Very good. I could use someone like you. If you pay attention and let old Arnie handle things, you could wind up very wealthy, very quickly."

"Oh, I don't know," Mac replied. "I don't think I'd like those Russian winters. Brrr."

Arnie laughed. "How about a Pacific paradise? I have just recently purchased property on an island that is quite beautiful and quite secluded. But with all the amenities. Resorts, surfing—" he looked at Melanie "—private beaches."

His insinuations made Melanie's palms itch with the desire to slap the smirk off his face. She tried to think of what else she could ask him, but there didn't seem to be anything.

Melanie glanced at Mac. Wasn't the cavalry supposed to come charging over the hill now? As she gazed questioningly into his ebony eyes, she saw that he, too, had expected the entrance of the guys in the white hats. What if no one was there? What if something had gone wrong and they were on their own?

"Well," Arnie was saying, "you don't mind if I check it before giving you the money, do you?"

Mac saw the fear in Melanie's eyes and tried to give her a reassuring look. It was a nice thought, but Melanie was still terrified.

Arnie let the disk sway between his forefinger and thumb for a few seconds before he sat down again. He drew the briefcase onto his lap and opened it. Melanie felt herself go cold. Inside the briefcase were several stacks of hundred dollar bills, but next to them was a portable personal computer.

As Arnie set the screen and flipped the little machine on, Melanie looked at Mac. There was alarm in the dark depths of his eyes, but not panic, and that reassured her for some reason. As Arnie slipped the disk into the drive, Mac looked casually over his shoulder at the thug guarding the balcony exit. The other thug was a few rows behind Arnie and on the other side, preventing escape via that exit. Melanie swallowed and hoped that Mac was good in a crisis, because this was definitely a crisis. She also hoped that he had thought of something to do, because she couldn't get her frazzled brain to think about anything but impending doom.

Arnie busily typed on his little keyboard. Then he stopped. Then he stared. And began turning red. Apparently wondering at his uncharacteristic silence, the first henchman took a few steps down the aisle.

"Is everything all right?"

Arnie snapped the computer off. "No, everything is not all right. These two have been playing us for fools. And that is unfortunate, because my friends, Mr. Smith and Mr. Jones, were hoping that something like this would occur. You see, they may not be subtle, but they are very thorough."

Smith, or maybe it was Jones, came several steps closer down the aisle, wearing a smile that Melanie could only call maniacal. They were going to be tortured! She didn't think she'd be able to stand up under something like that. Not that it mattered, because even if she told them where the disk was, it wouldn't do them any good—they couldn't get it. Then she reasoned that they weren't necessarily after the disk—just the information about how Mac had hidden the file. But, as she watched the approach of Mr. Smith, she didn't think he would care who had the information or where it was.

As she stood mentally wringing her hands, Mr. Smith approached Mac from the side. Suddenly, Mac whirled and kicked the gun out of the man's hand. Karate! Why hadn't Melanie taken those lessons at the Y?

"Melanie, run!"

Mac's request was about to be heeded when Melanie saw Mr. Jones approaching.

"Don't kill them!" Arnie yelled. "We need the code for the file!"

Melanie was glad that Arnie didn't want them dead, but she also knew that it wasn't a pardon but a postponement. As Mr. Jones smiled at her and reached for her arm, she backed up and let her purse strap slide off her shoulder and into her hand. Then she swung it with everything she had at the menacing face before her.

He looked surprised for the brief second before the weight of the purse slammed against his head. The paperweights crashed against the bookends inside the purse, and Melanie felt the weight of the purse swing back to hit her thigh. The man's eyes rolled upward, and he sank, unconscious, to the floor.

Melanie hoped he wasn't dead as she picked up Jones's gun and flung it over the railing. She then turned to run the opposite way.

It was then that she heard a rumble, then, suddenly, there were people everywhere. Melanie could see men with guns behind Mac, and she could hear more men taking up positions down in the auditorium. She and Mac had been rescued! The cavalry had arrived after all. Melanie started to smile with relief when her arm was encircled by a steely grip. Arnie!

He had stepped over the two rows of seats and was directly behind her. To their right was the exit. To their left was the railing, and beyond that was a twenty-foot drop.

She felt herself being pulled back against Arnie's thin body, and, as she looked at Mac's drawn face, she saw a knife.

It was a switchblade, about four inches long. At first he pointed it in Mac's direction, but, then he slowly moved it to rest alongside the beating jugular of Melanie's throat.

"Now," Arnie said, very softly, but clearly, "shall we begin again?"

Mac drew a deep breath, but didn't let it out. It was released as he spoke, his own words sounding much more threatening to Melanie than Arnie's.

"You hurt her, Edwards, and I swear there won't be room on the planet for you to hide."

"Oh, but there is, Chandler. A place where, should you manage to get in, you'd never be able to get out."

"I don't think *you* understand, Edwards. I don't care what happens after. But I can and I will be able to find you. No matter what, no matter where. Now, let her go."

Melanie could almost feel Arnie's indecision. She was holding her breath for fear that the cold steel blade that was resting against her throat would slip.

She thought she heard another voice, someone telling Arnie to let the woman go. For some reason, Melanie's hearing didn't work too well, and the order to Arnie to drop the knife sounded strangely distant. Then she was released. She heard Arnie speaking to Mac.

"Looks like I lose. But, since I always was a poor sport, I'll make your victory shallow."

Melanie felt Arnie's hand in the middle of her back, and suddenly she was sailing over the rail.

She closed her eyes, expecting to be crunched on the iron of the seat backs, but, instead, felt a sharp tug on her shoulder. The strap of her purse had caught on the railing. She maintained a grip on the body of the purse. She clasped her hands tightly around the leather bag and dangled, terrified of letting go.

She could hear scuffling going on on the balcony, then she heard Mac's voice.

"Hang on, Melanie!"

She opened her eyes and looked up. The strap of the purse was caught on a nail protruding from the railing. Melanie wondered what it was for. Then she wondered why she wasn't thanking the powers that be for its existence. She was still hearing a lot of commotion. People were talking and shouting and running around. Melanie was considering if it wouldn't be easier to climb back up to the balcony when she heard something quite clearly out of all the other noises.

The stitching on the leather strap of the purse was beginning to tear. It wouldn't hold much longer. It was then that she heard his voice. Only it was below her now.

"Melanie, let go."

What? Was he crazy?

"I don't think that's such a good idea, Mac."

"Yes, it is. Trust me, I'll catch you."

"Promise?"

"Cross my heart and hope to die."

Melanie released the purse and felt herself fall, but not for long. She crashed into Mac's body, and they both fell to the floor, between a row of seats. He had broken her fall, and she had knocked the breath out of him. As he lay there, wheezing, she thought that he was the most beautiful sight in the world and commenced kissing him and laughing.

"I fell for you! Do you get it?"

Mac nodded. "You're hysterical," he gasped.

"Well, thanks," she said, "I think you're pretty funny, too."

When his breathing returned to normal, he struggled to sit up. "Sweetheart, are you sure you're all right?"

Melanie nodded. She still felt slightly dazed and maybe a little light-headed, but she was hearing clearly again and her sense of touch was perfect.

"I'm fine," she said, her fingers locked behind his neck. "But I'm stuck on you."

"I feel the same about you, Melanie, but I think—"

She giggled. "No, I mean it. The goop from the floor is all over us. My hands are stuck on your neck."

Mac grinned. "Well, we'll see about getting them off— later. Much later."

He leaned forward, and she met his lips with her own.

Melanie heard a voice calling from the back of the theater.

"Sorry we didn't come in sooner, but we didn't want to let them hear us and panic. Melanie, those were great clues... say, where'd you go?" Then Kyle's voice came closer.

"Hey! What're you doing on the floor? You know better than that. What would Mom say if she saw you?"

Kyle leaned over them from the next aisle, with Nancy peeking over his shoulder.

"Don't you people know that there are statements to be made, depositions to be taken, bad guys to be fingerprinted, a helluva interesting tape to listen to—"

Melanie and Mac looked up at him reluctantly.

"Ssshhh!"

Kyle then watched his older brother resume his blatant activity. He and Nancy shrugged and sat down. Nancy looked at the blank movie screen.

"Focus!"

"The least they could do is give us money for popcorn."

Chapter Ten

Melanie was still a little overawed by what they had been through and about who was involved. She stole a glance at Mac's strong profile while they were sitting in Nancy's living room several hours later. She suddenly had the definite impression that he knew that she was looking at him, but he didn't acknowledge her scrutiny with so much as a blink of his dark eyes.

She wondered just what he was capable of doing. She had witnessed his relentless pursuit of the hard facts to incriminate those people who were guilty of being traitors, and he had told her that he had been working toward this goal for almost a year. He had given up his military career and almost lost his life. She shuddered now to think that she had almost lost him.

She had experienced so much in the past week that she wasn't sure about anything anymore. Just last week she had been a rather carefree, independent photojournalist. Her main interest had been which lens filter to use and the date of the next family get-together at Liane's house. Now, a scant week later, her whole life had been changed, her priorities reordered.

Now, her first priority was this handsome, enigmatic man. Everything else in her life paled in comparison. She thought about what it would be like if he left, and she felt a coldness gripping her heart.

Melanie knew nothing about having a serious relationship. She felt inadequate and awkward. What was she supposed to do? What should she say? How could she make him stay with her?

A sadness enveloped her. She couldn't make Mac stay, and she couldn't force him to ask her to go with him back to Salem. He had to choose to be with her. And if he did want to be with her—in Salem—would she want to leave Bayview?

She didn't even need to contemplate that last question. If Mac asked her to go with him to the jungles of Borneo, Melanie's only question would be "When do we leave?" Now, as she sat watching as the last of the federal agents left her best friend's house, she sighed a temporary sigh of relief.

Melanie and Mac had been giving statements and depositions to the FBI for hours. A quick glance at the cuckoo clock told Melanie it was four-thirty in the morning. Kyle had left two hours earlier to escort the prisoners to the federal jail in Salem. He had promised to call with a report as soon as possible.

Melanie felt tired, but her mind didn't want to shut down. Nancy had conked out at four o'clock, barely making it to her bedroom before collapsing. Mac didn't seem to be affected at all by the exhaustion that was threatening to claim her. Except for the faint lines etched near his eyes and mouth, no one would guess what he had been through in the past twenty-four hours. Melanie longed to wrap her arms around him and tell him that she loved him and that every-thing was going to be okay. But she didn't. She wasn't sure he would want to hear about her love.

The fact that they had really only met a week ago was partially to blame for causing her to hesitate when she would have blurted out her feelings for him and asked how he felt. She was afraid to confront him. Afraid to get a response she didn't want. A response that would hurt her.

Half of the time they had spent together had been when he didn't even know who he was. She hadn't met his par-ents or his friends. And if his relationship with Kyle was anything to judge by, their family was close. As close as her own.

She knew what she wanted. She wanted Mac to ask her to marry him. She wanted them to live happily ever after. Un-fortunately, she also knew that all that was a dream. Fan-tasy. Mac's words to Kyle entered her conscious again, despite her efforts to chase them away. He had laughed off the idea of marriage as if it were ludicrous. If she thought about it rationally, Melanie had to agree that it did seem il-logical. But she wasn't interested in logic now. She had never felt so connected to any man, and she was afraid of losing him.

Her brow crinkling, she wondered if he was even hers to lose. Kyle had asked Mac about someone named Liz. Who was she? More importantly, who was she to Mac?

Melanie rubbed her eyes wearily and laid her head back on the cushions of the sofa. Just a few minutes of rest, and then she would be fine. Then she would face Mac and ask him how he felt, tell him how much she loved him. Yes, she would talk with him in just a few...

Melanie didn't see the tender look on Mac's face as he gazed down at her sleeping face. She didn't see his look of decision as he hastily scrawled a note and put it on the cof-fee table. She felt herself floating in a dream, but didn't realize until later that it was Mac, carrying her to his car and settling her on the seat. The sound of the engine starting didn't wake her. She merely mumbled something about talking later and snuggled into a more comfortable position.

It was the absence of motion that caused Melanie to awake some time later. She blinked her large hazel eyes several times. The car was absolutely still and the silence was pervasive. Then, she realized that it really wasn't that quiet. She could hear the wind stirring the branches of the trees outside the car, and in the not too far distance, she could hear the waves of the Pacific crashing onto rocks on a beach far below where they were.

She should have felt disoriented, but she didn't. She knew where she was. She was with Mac.

She turned her head on the seat back cushion and saw Mac watching her, a strange expression on his face.

Melanie pushed her hands through her hair and sat up straight. She smiled a little self-consciously and noticed that the enigmatic expression on Mac's face had disappeared. He glanced out the front windshield and then back at her.

"We're here."

"Here? What do you mean? You should have woken me."

"I couldn't bring myself to disturb you. You're really beautiful when you're asleep." His voice was deep and hushed in the darkness of the car. The sun was just beginning to rise, casting pink and pale gold shadows over his face. Melanie laughed quietly.

"You mean because my mouth was shut?"

Now it was Mac's turn to laugh, but he, too, kept it low. "No, that's not what I meant. You're always beautiful, but in sleep you have a defenseless, childlike serenity. It makes me want to protect you."

She leaned over and kissed him gently, then stroked his cheek softly, looking past the shadows into his dark eyes. Then her eyes widened to take in their surroundings. She was sitting in Mac's Jaguar...she vaguely remembered some of the trip. She'd thought she was dreaming. Noticing how comfortable he looked at the wheel of the sports car, Melanie touched the dashboard tentatively.

"Has it been difficult being separated from your baby? Have you missed her terribly?"

Mac looked puzzled for a fraction of a second, then his expression turned to chagrin. He knew she was talking about his pampered automobile.

"I guess I have missed her. But not so much that she occupied my thoughts. That is the fault of another lady altogether."

Melanie's smile was shy, but pleased. She wished she could preserve the way she felt at that moment, and she wanted to believe that he felt the same way about her. She felt happy, but tentative. She had always thought that love would be the answer to everything, but now she wondered if love was really enough. Could those feelings continue without the excitement and danger from which they had sprung? Would Mac become bored with her? She hoped not, because she didn't know how she could ever be happy without him.

"What are you thinking about so intensely?"

The sound of his voice didn't startle her, rather, it seemed to cut through the fog of her inner musings like an expected beacon. She smiled mysteriously. "Oh, I don't think I should tell you. You'd only get a swelled head."

Then she turned and got out of the car, shutting the door as softly as she could so as not to disturb the relative silence and sense of peace that permeated their surroundings.

When she looked around her, Melanie was awed. Although it was still rather dark, the first rays of the sunrise

were filtering weakly through the branches of the trees sur-
rounding a house. She had an immediate impression of sol-
itude and peace and seclusion. She walked slowly toward the
house. Trees were all around her, around the house, shield-
ing it, lending it the appearance of being part of the landscape. She stopped to gaze up at the color-streaked sky
through the branches of the trees.

"Breathtaking, isn't it?"

Mac's voice was soft, barely above a whisper. Melanie
knew instinctively that this place was very important to him.
Maybe it was his own personal retreat. She nodded in unnecessary response to his question and was about to ask him
about the house when he stepped around her and inserted a
key in the lock, and then pushed lightly on the door.

As Melanie crossed the threshold into the house, Mac
flipped on a switch and the foyer was flooded with soft light.
For a split second, Melanie had the impression that she was
still outside. Then she blinked and realized that that was the
impression she was supposed to get. The house was really an
A-frame cabin with a loft. One huge room with tree trunks
for support pillars under the loft. An open kitchen was in
the back, and another door led to what Melanie ascer-
tained was the bathroom.

Everything was wood and stone. Melanie walked slowly
into the cabin and stood on a braided rug in front of a stone
fireplace like the one at her own cabin, only larger. This
fireplace stretched from floor to ceiling, and there was a
second fireplace in the loft.

The walls were paneled, and the base of the counter in the
kitchen appeared to be granite. She turned around slowly,
taking in everything and loving it all. It was so perfectly...in tune. Yes, that was it. The cabin and all of its
furnishings and interior design were in tune with its surroundings. As she completed the circle in her inspection, her
gaze fell on Mac, leaning casually against the doorframe.

As Melanie gazed at him, she realized that his casual stance was deceptive. He had been watching her. Now it seemed that he was waiting...for what? Then she knew. This was Mac's cabin. He had seen her getaway in the mountains and now she was seeing his getaway near the ocean.

Other things became apparent to her as she returned his stare. He had built this house; she knew he had. It was there, in those beautiful ebony eyes. Pride and protectiveness and...what? Melanie couldn't quite grasp the other emotion as it flitted through his eyes.

"It's beautiful, Mac. I want to say more, but somehow it would seem trite. The only word that comes to mind is *harmonious*."

"Harmonious?"

He hadn't moved, and he was still watching her.

Melanie nodded. "Yes. In harmony with its surroundings. It's like it belongs...it doesn't interrupt the natural setting. It contributes...blends..." She trailed off, feeling as if she wasn't getting through to him. Then she said, lamely, "You know what I mean?"

He pushed himself away from the doorframe then and closed the door. "Yes, I know. I just wasn't sure if anyone else would."

She smiled and wagged a finger at him. "You're being very mysterious, Wendell."

When he didn't respond to her use of his given name, she took a few steps toward him. "Hey, what's the matter? Why didn't you tell me not to call you Wendell?"

Before she was aware of what he was doing, he had seized her upper arms and hauled her against his hard, muscular chest. Melanie felt her breathing become erratic as she stared up at him with a wide hazel gaze. Then his grip on her softened, and he was running his powerful hands gently over the sensitive flesh of her arms. His eyes were boring into hers, and she had the feeling that he was asking her something, but wasn't voicing it. Then he was speaking, and it took Melanie a moment to hear his words and not just the sound of his voice.

"...was possible, but I like it when you say my name."

She smiled again, but this time she leaned into his body and wrapped her arms around his neck. Standing on tiptoe, she brushed her lips against his, then pulled back just enough so that she could speak.

"I'm glad. Because sometimes I like calling you Wendell. And I didn't want you to not like something I like."

Mac grinned at her illogical logic and looped his arms around her waist.

"Oh, I think we like a lot of the same things."

Melanie sighed in agreement as his lips touched hers. She was beginning to grow accustomed to these feelings of electrically charged emotions whenever Mac touched her. Sometimes just when he looked at her.

All too soon, he was pulling away from her. Sighing into her hair, he held her close to him for a few moments, then he stepped back. "Melanie, we have to talk—to get certain things straightened out."

When she stared blankly at him, he muttered an oath and raked his fingers through his hair. Melanie didn't like the feel of this. This felt like the buildup to a rejection. No, she didn't like this at all. Looking around for an escape, her eyes fell on the telephone hanging on the wall in the kitchen.

"Did Kyle call from Salem before we left? I don't remember...."

Mac's eyes looked relieved—too relieved for Melanie. "No, I told Nancy we'd call from here and find out what he said." Melanie nodded and walked gratefully toward the telephone. Every moment she could stall prolonged her time with Mac.

After rapidly punching out the familiar series of numbers, she waited. After four rings, her brow furrowed. Mac, who had been leaning against the counter, stood up straight and looked at her.

"Hello?"

The breathy, unsteady voice was right, but not right.

"Nancy?" Melanie said tentatively. "What's wrong?"

There was a pause. Melanie could have sworn her friend was taking a deep breath. Nancy had never taken a deep breath in her life.

"Nothing is wrong. Where are you?"

Melanie was still confused, but shrugging at Mac. "We're at Mac's house."

"Right. Were you surprised?" Now Nancy sounded like herself.

"Yes, sort of. Did Kyle call you from Salem?"

There was a pause on the other end of the line. "Uh, yeah...I mean..."

Melanie stared at the telephone receiver before putting it back to her ear. If she didn't know better, she would say that Nancy was flustered. But Nancy didn't get flustered. She had never been flustered. Melanie wondered if her friend had been into the cooking sherry.

"Nancy, what is it? Are you all right?"

Mac was tapping Melanie's shoulder, and she was waving him off.

"What?"

Melanie was exasperated. "What is wrong with you, Nancy Doyle?"

Then Melanie heard whispering. And a giggle. Nancy Doyle never giggled.

"Umm, nothing is wrong. What was it you wanted to know?"

"Kyle. Kyle Chandler. Has he called you? Geez, Nancy, was your brain stolen by an alien horde or what?"

"I beg your pardon. Yes."

"Yes, what?"

"Yes, he called."

"What did he say?"

There was more talking in the background. "He says that he would like to speak to Mac."

"Ohh," Melanie said with a sigh. So Kyle was there. "They're pretty lethal, aren't they, Nance?"

"And how," was the short response.

Melanie handed the phone to Mac and stood aside. He took it from her with a scowl on his handsome face.

"What did the attorney general say?...What about the pictures?...Oh...Good...What did the general say?...Uh-huh...What about Major Eastman?...Damn...Right, maybe...The cliff...Maybe...Shut up...You'd better not, Kyle...Well, yeah...I'll do it myself!...You're lucky I can't get you through this phone, little brother...Yeah, right...Thanks...Bye."

Melanie stared at Mac, curiosity burning through her. What kind of a conversation was that? She didn't have any idea what was said, and everything Mac had said was cryptic, to say the least.

"What is it? What did he say?" she asked.

"Nothing, really. He and Joe took Edwards and his friends to Salem, and the attorney general of Oregon is fighting with the Washington people over who gets to prosecute. I think that there is enough for everybody to get a piece of old Arnie."

"And?" she prompted.

He glanced at her quickly, then shrugged. "Uh, the pictures you took helped convince Mr. Smith to rat on Mr. Jones, and he detailed his involvement in exchange for a lighter sentence."

"What else?"

Mac sighed at her insistence and continued. "General Treanor has been informed of what happened and is...satisfied. Except for the fact that Major Eastman is still on that island. They won't be able to get him unless he leaves. Kyle thinks that he will. Sooner or later."

She nodded as she considered his explanation. "What cliff?"

He smiled and shook his head. "This cliff." He pointed through the windows of the living room, and Melanie saw that the house was, indeed, built on a cliff overlooking the Pacific Ocean.

"What about the other stuff? About doing it yourself and—"

"That's a surprise."

Sighing, Melanie shook her head and gazed at him. "Both of you are too mysterious. Does it run in your family?"

Mac grinned and shrugged.

Melanie leaned back and sighed. "Apparently that isn't the only thing that runs in the family."

"What is that...oh, yeah." He chuckled softly. "At first I wondered what was wrong when you were talking with Nancy. Agents aren't supposed to get sidetracked like that."

Melanie smiled. "It doesn't look as if any of us were doing what we were supposed to do."

He didn't say anything, but took her hand in his, lacing his fingers through hers. He pulled her toward him and held her hands between them, slowly moving his thumbs along her knuckles. His voice was hardly more than a whisper when he finally spoke. "Melanie...I—we have to talk." He didn't really sound as if he wanted to talk.

She wanted to say no. But that wouldn't be very mature. She felt a certain dread at his words. He looked uncomfortable. It was as if he had to say something he didn't want to say. Melanie swallowed a lump in her throat. She was sure she didn't want to hear whatever it was, either.

Melanie told herself that if she were a mature adult in an enlightened society, she would just sit down and talk with Mac and ask him what he felt about their future and what it held. She acknowledged to herself that she was too afraid of what Mac might say to venture that kind of discussion. What if he avoided her eyes and began a well-we've-had-a-lot-of-fun-but speech? She didn't think she would be able to handle it.

When she didn't say anything, but continued to stare blankly at him, Mac released her and took a couple of steps toward the kitchen, then stopped and seemed to reflect on the living-room area. Melanie wondered why he seemed so torn. Surely it was rather easy for him. He knew that she loved him. Didn't he? She hadn't mentioned her feelings again after that day at the cabin because she felt that he needed more time to figure out his own feelings.

She realized she hadn't wanted the case to be solved because as long as there was a case, she had had Mac right there beside her, but without it, she wasn't sure where she stood. He had made a commitment to protect her while there was danger, but now that she was safe, what did he want?

And Mac's words at her cabin were ever present in her mind. He had said he was crazy about her—whatever that meant—then he'd told his brother that the idea of marrying her was ridiculous since they'd only just met, and then he'd told her she belonged to him. Now, when she thought that he'd only brought her here to tell her goodbye, she felt a strange sadness. She also felt a bit angry. She wished he'd just say it, so she wouldn't have to worry about what he was going to say.

Melanie looked up at Mac, his brow furrowed in thought. His eyes widened as he saw her watching him. She wondered if she would be able to speak to him, to look at him without demanding to know exactly what he wanted of her. Keeping her voice low, she asked, "What do you want to talk about?"

Mac still didn't move. His voice was even when he answered. "Well, I think that there are a lot of things we need to discuss. Why, were you thinking of something in particular?"

Melanie's brows drew together. Was he nervous? Mac? She didn't think she'd ever seen him nervous. Not even when Arnie had threatened her. He had been furious, but not nervous. This new side of him was making her uneasy. Why didn't he just get it over with?

"No," she said, softly. "I wasn't thinking of anything in particular."

Mac raked his fingers through his dark hair and sighed. "You must be tired. Why don't we put off talking until after we've had something to eat and a chance to rest?"

She blinked at him owlishly. He was obviously trying to avoid a conversation he didn't want to have. To Melanie that meant only one thing: he was leaving and didn't want her to come with him. He didn't love her.

Walking slowly past him, she looked through the windows of the sliding door. Opening the door, she walked onto a redwood deck. She heard him call her name, but continued on. He might not be comfortable telling her it was over, but she was more desperate to avoid hearing his words.

There was a railing all around the deck, with steps leading down to the ground. She went down the steps and then started down a path, scraping her hands on bushes as she scrambled down the steep hill toward the beach. Thoughts of the past week flashed through her mind.

They had started an explosive relationship based on the passion born of a mutual attraction and the danger that heightened everything they did. But now it was over, and she needed time to think. Maybe it wasn't as bad as it felt. It couldn't be.

Fighting a losing battle for control of her emotions, Melanie didn't notice Mac following her onto the beach, nor did she see the hand extending to touch her shoulder.

It was an instinctive reaction on her part to jerk back, turning her tortured eyes to his for a split second. She saw surprise, then concern.

"Melanie—" he started, then fell silent. Melanie took a deep breath. She knew she should talk with him, but she didn't want to be so close to him while he rejected her.

She began to step away, but his hand shot out to grasp her upper arm.

"No, Melanie. Not this time." His voice was quiet but laced with steel. Melanie shrugged.

"I wasn't going anywhere," she said flatly.

Mac saw the resignation in her eyes and felt the slight change in her stance. He released her arm, but not her eyes.

"Now," he began, raking his fingers through his wind-blown hair, "will you please tell me what is wrong?"

Melanie remained mute, unable to look away, but also unable to speak.

"Okay," he said, undeterred by her lack of cooperation. "How about if I ask the questions and you just nod or shake your head?"

He was attempting a teasing and light tone, but Melanie couldn't bring herself to smile. Why didn't he just get it over with? Why didn't he just say that he was sorry, but that he had realized he wasn't ready to make a commitment and that it had been swell, but . . .

Mac, still getting no response from her, tried again. "Melanie, we are not going anywhere until you tell me what is wrong. I'll wait all day if I have to."

He looked so concerned that Melanie couldn't stand it. She looked away, toward the ocean. If he was being sympathetic and kind out of pity, she wouldn't be able to bear it. But she knew she had to say something because he was not going to stop badgering her. Now was as bad a time as any.

"Why?" she asked, trying to will away the tremor in her voice. She stepped away from him, her eyes still on the horizon.

"Why what?" He was still staring at her face, but Melanie couldn't bring herself to look at him.

"Why did you bring me here?" She closed her eyes against the impact of the words she knew she would hear.

He didn't say anything for a moment, then he jammed his hands into his pockets and followed her gaze, taking in the gray sky over the ocean.

"I wanted us to talk about what's happened between us, and...I also wanted to tell you a few things that I didn't tell you before."

Melanie forced herself to take a deep breath. She was not going to cry. At least not until she was alone. "You really don't have to do this, Mac."

"I don't?"

"No. I think I know what you're going to say, and it's okay. I appreciate your concern for my feelings, but you didn't have to bring me all the way down here just to let me know you aren't interested in me."

The silence shook her composure more than anything he might have said. After a minute, she finally found the courage to turn and look at him.

Mac was gaping at her, his black eyes wide with disbelief. Suddenly, he reached out and grabbed her shoulders, pulling her close to him. "Is that what you thought?"

Confused as much by his nearness as his words, Melanie merely nodded. He shook her gently and laughed. "I was scared to death that you wouldn't want to be with me anymore, Melanie. Why do you think that I practically kidnapped you in your sleep and brought you down here with me?"

Hearing his words almost made Melanie cry again, but instead, she blinked away the moisture and smiled. "Mac, I thought you knew how I felt. I told you at the cabin that I was falling in love with you."

He shrugged. "I wanted to give you time to decide if it was me or just the atmosphere."

Now, Melanie gaped. "Atmosphere? Oh, you must mean the romance of wondering whether or not someone was going to kill us? Or maybe the glamour of hiding out in a cabin with no electricity? Or the excitement of a leaky canoe? No, I suppose you're right. It couldn't have been you. It must have been the atmosphere."

When he had the grace to look sheepish, she said softly, "Wendell, I think I started falling in love with you the first time I met you at WilCom. I had been intrigued with the stranger in town before that, but when I saw you that day, I was overwhelmed by feelings. And I'm still overwhelmed. I love you, Mac."

His hands framed her face, her eyes wide with hope. "Melanie, I love you, too. I was afraid that my love wouldn't be enough."

"Believe me, Mac," she said softly, "I love you enough for anything. And knowing that you love me is all I'll ever need."

He smiled down into her face and then lowered his lips to hers. The kiss was full of love and promise and wanting. He slanted his mouth over hers, and Melanie parted her lips for him. The hunger in him thrilled her, and she pressed closer to him.

He slowly pulled away from her. "Look, sweetheart, we really do have to talk. It's important."

"All right," she said, smiling up at him. "But whatever it is won't change the way I feel about you."

"I hope not." He looked down the beach and, taking Melanie's hand, began walking. "I, uh, wasn't exactly truthful about everything, Melanie."

She nodded absently and looked over at him. "I suspected that much. I didn't expect to be told everything. As a matter of fact, I was surprised that you and Kyle didn't send Nancy and me out of town."

He laughed. "We couldn't have done that. You knew too much. Besides, we liked having you where we could keep an eye on you. No, it wasn't about what happened, exactly."

Melanie stopped and faced him. "Mac, what is it?"

"I, uh, told you that I had been in the army and that I was now a private computer consultant in Salem."

"So?"

"Well, I am and I'm not." When she began to protest, he held up a hand. "I know. I'm getting to it. I'm not a private consultant, and I don't live in Salem...well, I did...but not since I joined the army."

"I don't understand," she said. "If you don't live there...what about your business card? It was in your wallet."

He nodded. "I know. It was part of my cover. I was supposed to have left the army in a huff and started my own company."

"Didn't you?"

"No. Actually, I'm still in the army. General Treanor and I set the whole thing up so that I could operate as a civilian to find out who was behind the computer break-ins. We kept as close to the truth as possible. That way there are fewer slipups. I do plan on opening my own consulting business when I retire. But that won't be for another ten or fifteen years."

Melanie was speechless for a moment, then her mind snapped back into place. "Why didn't you tell me?"

He looked away and then took her hand to continue walking. "At first, it was just easier. If anyone asked you, you could have told them truthfully that you thought I was a private businessman."

"What about later?"

"Later, when I knew how I felt about you, I wasn't sure how you'd feel about living the life of an army wife. It can be really difficult, Melanie, and I don't make that much money."

Melanie's eyebrows shot up, and her mouth dropped open. Had she misunderstood him? "Just a second. I think my hearing is on the fritz. An army—what?"

Mac grinned, his eyes hopeful. "I told you I love you, Melanie. I want you to marry me...that would make you an army wife."

Her mind was reeling. She had been so terrified about the reasons behind his talk. Now he was saying he wanted to get married! "At the cabin, you told Kyle that it was too soon, the idea of marriage—"

"Forget what I told Kyle." He grinned sheepishly. "I was just trying to be cool around my little brother."

"Cool! You made me crazy because you wanted to be 'cool'!"

"Hey, I'm sorry. I didn't think I meant that much to you," he joked.

"Just for that," she said, "I will marry you. And you'll never be cool again."

Then Mac kissed her, and she melted against him for a moment before pulling back and gliding her fingers over his jawline. "Mac, where do you live, if you don't live in Salem?"

He smiled. "Right now, Seattle. But that could change, darling. I could be stationed anywhere in the world. Could you see yourself wandering around the world like that?"

"As long as I'm with you, Wendell, I'll be deliriously happy. Maybe I could write some articles about life overseas for some magazines."

His face was suddenly serious. "You have to be sure, Melanie. I don't think I could stand it if you married me and then couldn't live the life of an army wife."

"Mac," she said gently. "I love you. And I wouldn't be happy anywhere unless I was with you. All that matters to me is that we're together. Maybe we could have a couple of little army brats to keep us company."

Suddenly she was being twirled around in his arms. "I love you, Melanie Rogers—soon to be Melanie Chandler!"

"And I love you, Wendell MacAuley Chandler," she murmured against his lips. "There was never any doubt about it."

*　*　*　*　*

COMING NEXT MONTH

#688 FATHER CHRISTMAS—Mary Blayney
Daniel Marshall had never thought he could have it all: his
precious daughters *and* the woman who'd given them a mother's
love. But Annie VerHollan believed in Christmas miracles....

#689 DREAM AGAIN OF LOVE—Phyllis Halldorson
Mary Beth Warren had left her husband, Flynn, upon discovering
the truth behind their vows. Now that they had a second chance,
could she risk dreaming again of love?

#690 MAKE ROOM FOR NANNY—Carol Grace
Maggie Chisholm planned to faithfully abide by her nanny
handbook. But the moment she laid eyes on Garrett Townsend
she broke the golden rule—by falling in love with her boss!

#691 MAKESHIFT MARRIAGE—Janet Franklin
Practical Brad Williamson had proposed to Rachel Carson purely
for the sake of her orphaned niece and nephew. But how long
could Rachel conceal her longing for more than a
makeshift marriage?

#692 TEN DAYS IN PARADISE—Karen Leabo
Carrie Bishop arrived in St. Thomas seeking adventure and found
it while hunting for treasure with Jack Harrington. But she
never counted on the handsome loner being her most
priceless find....

#693 SWEET ADELINE—Sharon De Vita
Adeline Simpson had gone to Las Vegas to find her grandfather
and bring him back home. Could casino owner Mac Cole
convince lovely Addy that she was missing a lot more?

AVAILABLE THIS MONTH:

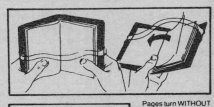
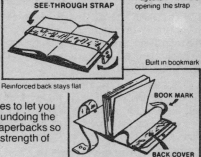

Available now from

SILHOUETTE®

Desire™

TAGGED #534
by Lass Small

Fredricka Lambert had always believed in true love, but she couldn't figure out whom to love... until lifelong friend Colin Kilgallon pointed her in the right direction—toward himself.

Fredricka is one of five fascinating Lambert sisters. She is as enticing as each one of her four sisters, whose stories you have already enjoyed.

- Hillary in GOLDILOCKS AND THE BEHR (Desire #437)

- Tate in HIDE AND SEEK (Desire #453)

- Georgina in RED ROVER (Desire #491)

- Roberta in ODD MAN OUT (Desire #505)

Don't miss the last book of this enticing miniseries, only from Silhouette Desire.

Wonderful, luxurious gifts can be yours with proofs-of-purchase from any specially marked "Indulge A Little" Harlequin or Silhouette book with the Offer Certificate properly completed, plus a check or money order (do not send cash) to cover postage and handling payable to Harlequin/Silhouette "Indulge A Little, Give A Lot" Offer. We will send you the specified gift.

Mail-in-Offer

OFFER CERTIFICATE

Item:	A. Collector's Doll	B. Soaps in a Basket	C. Potpourri Sachet	D. Scented Hangers
# of Proofs-of-Purchase	18	12	6	4
Postage & Handling	$3.25	$2.75	$2.25	$2.00
Check One				

Name _____

Address _____ Apt. # _____

City _____ State _____ Zip _____

ONE PROOF OF PURCHASE

To collect your free gift by mail you must include the necessary number of proofs-of-purchase plus postage and handling with offer certificate.

SR-2

Harlequin®/Silhouette®

Mail this certificate, designated number of proofs-of-purchase and check or money order for postage and handling to:

INDULGE A LITTLE
P.O. Box 9055
Buffalo, N.Y. 14269-9055